BREAKING
THE
STORY

ALSO BY ASHLEY FARLEY

BREAKING THE STORY

To Arlene —
I hope this will
be a nice break from
real-life politics!

ASHLEY FARLEY

XOXO,
Ashley

Copy right@2016 by Ashley Farley

Cover design: damonza.com
Formatting: damonza.com
Editor: Patricia Peters at A Word Affair LLC

Leisure Time Books, a division of AHF Publishing

ISBN for ePub: 978-0-9861672-4-9
ISBN for Print: 978-0-9861672-5-6

For Cameron and Ned

1

SEVERE THUNDERSTORMS HAD threatened much of the East Coast for most of the afternoon. Flights were delayed at all the major airports, many of them canceled until the following morning. After a turbulent flight and rough landing, Scottie was anxious to disembark the cramped airplane and head home to a hot bath and a big glass of red wine. For the past three days, she'd been covering the Republican National Convention in Cleveland. The master of ceremonies' voice still reverberated in her head, and her vision's spectrum was now limited to three colors—red, white, and blue. She was not enthusiastic about having to repeat the process for the Democratic convention in less than a week.

Scottie flung her camera bag over her shoulder and wheeled her carry-on suitcase through the crowded terminal, down the escalator, and out into the sultry afternoon. Steam rose off the pavement from the recent rain, and the earth smelled like stewed garbage. A couple streaks of lightning lit up the dark sky, followed by rumbling thunder. As she darted across the road to the parking deck, she noticed a bank of clouds rolling in from the west, the promise for a stormy evening ahead. She located her car in the same aisle on the same level where she always parked. She popped her hatch and was stowing her luggage in the back when she noticed her rear passenger tire was flat.

"Damn it!" Her voiced bounced off the concrete floor and ceiling of the parking deck. When the image of her AAA bill lying unopened and past due on her desk came to mind, she slumped back against the car. "This is great, just great. A perfect ending to a miserable trip."

Removing her cell phone from the pocket of her raincoat, she punched in her husband's number. She wasn't surprised when the call went straight to voice mail. She'd been trying to reach him all afternoon, but he hadn't responded to any of her voice or text messages.

She was too distracted with her phone to notice a man approaching until he was right in front of her. "That's rotten luck. Can I help you?" he asked, the concern in his voice sounding sincere.

Scottie recognized him from her earlier flights—both the one from Cleveland to Chicago then into Richmond. He was tall, over six feet, with a sandy crew cut and gray eyes. He appeared harmless enough in his conservative suit and capped-toe shoes. Even so, Scottie wasn't in the habit of talking to strangers.

"No, but thanks. My husband will be out in a minute. He's collecting our luggage from the baggage claim." Avoiding his gaze, she gestured toward the terminal.

He rubbed his chin, seemingly perplexed. "That's funny. I noticed you on the plane. I got the impression you were traveling alone."

So he'd noticed her just as she'd noticed him.

Careful Scottie, she told herself. *Remember you're a married woman.*

He continued to rub his chin. "Unless, of course, the

2

three-hundred-pound black man who was sitting next to you is your husband."

She threw up her hands. "Okay, you busted me. Nothing wrong with a girl trying to protect herself from the advances of strange men."

"As you should, but I promise you don't need protection from me. I'm as harmless as they come." He held his hand out to her. "I'm Guy Jordan."

"Guy? You're name is really Guy, as in *that* guy."

"That's me—the *guy* everybody loves to hate."

"Ha-ha." She squeezed and released his hand. "I'm Scottie Darden. It's nice to meet you."

His gaze traveled back to the flat tire. "Now that we've been officially introduced, are you comfortable with me changing your tire, or do you want to wait for your *husband* to come?" he asked with a hint of sarcasm in his voice and a little smirk playing along his lips.

"Trust me, I have a husband. He's just not answering his phone right now." She waved her phone at him before shoving it into her back pocket. Turning her back on Guy, she began to remove her bags from the back of the car. "How hard can changing a tire be anyway?" she asked, lifting the hatch on the compartment that concealed her spare.

"Not hard at all when you drive a Matchbox." His genuine smile brightened his face. "Why don't I hold the car up while you change the tire? We won't even need to use the jack."

She held up a black metal diamond-shaped tool. "Is that what this is?"

"On second thought, you'd better let me handle this." He took the jack from her and set it on the ground beside the flat tire. Slipping out of his suit jacket, he rolled up the sleeves on his starched white button-down shirt. "Now, if you'll hand me the owner's manual from the glove compartment…"

She reached for the door handle, and then stopped herself when she realized he was teasing her. "Are you always this fresh with married women you encounter in parking decks?"

"Only the pretty ones."

She furrowed her brow. "There you go again."

"I'm sorry. I didn't mean to make you uncomfortable. I totally respect the fact that you're married. No more teasing, I promise." He set the jack under the frame near the flat tire and pumped up the car. "How much did you pay for this go-kart anyway, a buck ninety-nine?"

She ran her hand over the roof of her Mini Cooper. "I'll have you know, I just traded my 4Runner for this fuel-conserving, high-performance machine."

"Why would you do that with gas prices at an all-time low?" he asked, as he loosened the lug nuts.

"We have the ozone layer to consider, you know. I'm guessing you drive a Suburban."

"I live in DC. I don't own a car."

Washington, huh? So he'd been in Cleveland attending the convention just as she'd suspected. His muscular body filled out his suit better than any politician she'd ever met. "Did the airline reroute you to Richmond because of the weather?"

"Yep. The storms are more severe the farther north you go. Washington, Baltimore, Philadelphia, they're all getting hit hard. I'll probably spend the night in Richmond, and drive back in the morning. Any chance I can shack up with you?" His expression was serious, but his gray eyes lightened with mischief.

Scottie burst out into laughter. "You're incorrigible. You know that?"

"That's what they tell me," he said with a wink.

They bantered back and forth while they worked. Scottie helped by handing him tools and holding the lug nuts. Within minutes, he'd swapped out the tires and secured the flat in the rear compartment.

"You can't go far on this spare. Fifty miles max." Removing a plaid linen handkerchief from his pocket, he mopped the sweat from his brow and then wiped the grease from his hands.

"I'll deal with it in the morning." She slammed the hatch shut and turned to him. "All kidding aside, I don't know how I can possibly thank you."

"I'm guessing your husband wouldn't approve of me buying you a drink."

"Brad would be grateful to you for helping me out of a bind. *I'm* the one who should buy *you* a drink, anyway." A loud rumble of thunder sounded in the distance. "But we should both get where we're going before the weather worsens."

"Okay, then. I hope our paths meet again someday."

"Seriously, Guy, thank you for coming to my rescue."

He bowed slightly at the waist. "The pleasure was all mine, m'lady." And with that, he slung his coat over his shoulder and wheeled his suitcase off toward the rental car lot.

2

RUSH HOUR TRAFFIC crawled through downtown Richmond, taking Scottie more than an hour to make what was usually a twenty-minute trip. By the time she pulled into the empty space behind her husband's silver Tahoe, in front of their row house on West Avenue in the Fan district, the rain was coming down in sheets. Pulling the hood of her raincoat over her head, she grabbed her bags from the back and made a dash for the door.

The lights were turned low in the living room, and candles flickered a soft glow from the mantle above the fireplace. Through the Sonos speakers stationed throughout the house, Al Green's deep sexy voice filled the rooms with songs from her romantic playlist, the one she reserved for lovemaking with Brad. If she'd been married to any other man, she would have assumed the candles and music were a romantic welcome home greeting. But Brad was not one for frivolous expressions of love, such as bringing her flowers or taking her out for dinner on their anniversary. The only candle she'd ever known him to use was the one in the bathroom he lit when he did his business.

She heard people talking upstairs—her husband's husky voice and the unmistakable sound of a woman giggling.

No wonder the bastard didn't answer his phone.

Fury burned in her chest and adrenaline pumped through her body.

How dare he light candles for another woman in my home.

Removing her camera from her camera bag, she adjusted the settings for indoor lighting and tiptoed up the stairs. Hugging the wall, she made her way past the nursery and down the hall to the master bedroom. She peeked around the doorjamb, and was stunned at the sight of a brunette beauty with bountiful breasts perched on top of her husband in their queen-size bed, the antique mahogany rice bed she'd slept in as a child, the one her parents gave them as a house-warming gift when they bought the house.

Bitch! Bastard!

Positioning her finger on the shutter, Scottie stepped inside the room and aimed the camera at them. "Say cheese!" She pressed the shutter and held it down. The camera snapped a continuous stream of photographs, capturing her husband's shocked expression and the woman's lips as they curled into a smug smile.

Shoving the woman aside, Brad made a move to get out of bed, but his feet got tangled in the sheets, and he fell to the floor. "I'm sorry, honey. I can explain," he said as he struggled to free his feet.

"No explanation needed." Scottie motioned at the brunette, who hadn't bothered to cover herself up. "The fact that you have a slut in my bed says it all." She snapped another photograph of her husband lying on the floor, helpless and hopeless. "A parting shot to remember you by. Definitely not your finest hour."

Scottie flew from the room and down the stairs. She grabbed her bags from the entry hall and hurried out to her car. She pounded the steering wheel. "That bastard!" she screamed. "How dare he cheat on me." When she noticed Brad standing in the doorway, she started her car and zoomed off down the road. Tears blinded her vision as she sped through the neighborhood backstreets toward the interstate.

She was halfway to her parents' farm in Goochland when she realized that running home to Mommy and Daddy was not the most grown-up way to respond to the crisis. She knew she could count on her parents' support. They hadn't liked Brad from the beginning, never seen the drive and determination that had initially attracted their daughter to the premed student from California. Barbara and Stuart Westport were not the type to say I told you so. They would wipe her tears with one hand while dialing the divorce attorney's office with the other. Her parents would be understanding, all right. Problem was, she wasn't ready to own up to her failure.

She whipped the Mini off the interstate and circled around to Broad Street, heading back toward downtown.

Scottie and Brad had gotten married a year after graduating from the University of Virginia. He'd taken a part-time job as a bartender to allow for more time to study for the MCAT. But that part-time soon became full-time with all thoughts of medical school forgotten. In the months since Christmas, Brad's take-home pay had dwindled to near nothing. When she questioned him, he claimed that business was slow, that the new hotspot around the corner on Shockhoe Slip had stolen their regular customers. She suspected her husband might be using drugs, but she had no way of proving it. While it hurt like hell to see him in bed with another woman, in many ways, Scottie felt relieved. Their relationship had been on a downward spiral for some time. Years even. She was tired of his empty promises. Tired of making excuses to her family and friends for his frequent absences at parties and family events. Tired of coming home after a long trip to find their house littered with beer bottles and dirty ashtrays.

Her cell phone lit up on the seat beside her, and Brad's name appeared across the screen. She reached for the phone and powered it off. The next time she communicated with him would be through an attorney.

Scottie contemplated her options for a place to spend the night. Already approaching the fifty-mile mark, she couldn't drive much farther on her spare tire. Her best friend, Anna, had been avoiding her since Christmas, since Scottie had inadvertently placed Anna's husband in danger of losing his medical license. The rest of her friends would undoubtedly be spending quiet weekends at home, nursing their babies and making love to their husbands. She could drive to Church Hill to her brother's house, where she knew she'd find a sympathetic shoulder to cry on. But Will would want all the details, and she wasn't ready to give voice to her drama. Tonight, she needed time alone to think. Tonight, she needed to drink tequila.

She took a right-hand turn onto the Boulevard, drove one block, and then turned left onto Franklin Street. She parked under the portico in front of the Jefferson Hotel, handed her key to the valet, and went inside to the front desk. After booking the cheapest room available, she wheeled her suitcase around the corner and rode the elevator to the third floor. The consolation prize to having the smallest room in the most luxurious hotel in the city was the stunning view overlooking downtown Richmond.

Scottie raked her hands through her tangled blonde curls and smeared clear gloss across her lips before making her way back down to the lobby. She found an empty seat at the bar and ordered a tequila martini from the muscled bartender. She took a long sip, savoring the burn and the warm afterglow.

She had every intention of drinking herself blind, then stumbling up to her room and hiding under the heavy comforter until check-out time at noon the next day, but she quickly tired of fending off advances from drunken men. Halfway through her second drink, she was ready to throw in the towel and go across the lobby to TJ's for a burger. And then *that guy* walked into the bar. Their eyes met and registered recognition.

This time when her heart did a little pitter-patter at the sight of his handsome face and strong body, she embraced it.

3

GUY NAVIGATED HIS way through the crowd to where Scottie was seated. "Well now, isn't this a coincidence?" he said.

She looked up from her martini. "Unless, of course, you're stalking me."

"Ouch. Hostile." He took a step back. "What happened to you in the hours since we last met?"

She jabbed at the olive with the pick in her martini. "Trust me, you don't want to know."

"Oh, but I do," he said, placing his hand over his heart. "The way I remember it, you owe me a drink for changing your tire. You even said you should buy it."

"All right, fine." When the woman next to her got up and left, Scottie extended an empty hand to the bar stool. "You might as well sit down. I'll buy you a drink. Then we'll be even."

Guy slid onto the bar stool and signaled the bartender. "I'll have a Dewars on the rocks. And bring the lady another of whatever she's having." He glanced down at her glass. "What *are* you having?"

"Tequila martinis. My third."

"Whoa. What's with the serious mood? You might as well tell me. I'll keep guessing until you do."

She drained the last of her drink and set the glass down on the bar. "Trust me, you don't want to hear this drama."

"Why don't you let me make that decision?"

She hesitated, unsure of whether she should confide her personal business to a man she barely knew. *Why not?* she finally decided. Maybe it would be easier to divulge her secret to a stranger.

"If you insist, but I warn you, it's not a pretty story. You're the first person I've told, so this isn't going to be easy. But here goes." Scottie placed her hands down on the bar to brace herself. "When I got home from the airport, I found my husband in bed with another woman. There. I said it out loud." She slumped back in her chair. "Which now makes it real."

His face filled with compassion. "That's the last thing I expected you to say. I'm so sorry, Scottie. Why are you sitting alone in a hotel bar? You should be with your family or friends."

"Because I needed some time to decompress. And I'm not alone anymore, anyway, now that you're here."

The bartender delivered their drinks and took away Scottie's empty glass. "Maybe talking it through with a stranger will help," Guy said.

"You helped me out of a bind this afternoon. I'd say that makes us more than strangers."

"You could've changed the tire yourself and you know it." He took a sip of his drink. "I can't imagine how hard it was for you to find your husband with another woman. Forgive me for prying, but did you suspect he was being unfaithful before now?"

"Not at all. Brad has plenty of flaws, but I never considered him the type who would cheat on his wife." She stirred her martini, lost in thought. "The truth is, I'm relieved. Our marriage hasn't worked for a long time."

"You're so young," Guy said. "Surely you haven't been married that long."

"I'm older than I look."

He raised an eyebrow. "I'd be willing to bet another round of drinks you haven't reached thirty yet."

"Signal the bartender, my friend, because I'm thirty and a half. Brad and I got married a year after we graduated from college."

His eyes widened. "I don't know anyone who gets married so young these days. Why not try living together first?"

"Because we were young and in love," Scottie said, biting back tears. "And if you're trying to make me feel better about the situation, it's not working. I'm well aware of my mistake." Scottie thought back to the early years of her marriage, when her husband's true colors were starting to show. "No doubt living together would've been the better option."

He squeezed her shoulder. "I didn't mean to hurt your feelings. The truth is, knowing people still commit to one another at such a young age restores my faith in the sanctity of marriage. Most unmarried couples I know either fight all the time or cheat on one another every chance they get. And I'm talking about people who are older than thirty."

"Must be something about the thirty-year age mark that makes people cheat."

Guy palmed his forehead. "I'm striking out here big time. That was insensitive of me, and I apologize."

The remorseful expression on his face didn't escape Scottie's notice. "It's okay, Guy. I know exactly what you mean. Our hookup culture has destroyed our generation's idea of marriage. Why make a commitment to someone when you can have friends with benefits? Call me old-fashioned, but I want a life partner, someone to raise a family with and grow old together."

"You'll find the right person. Don't give up on your dreams because your husband let you down."

"Easy for you to say. You didn't just find your wife in bed with another man."

"True." He stared into his drink, as though the amber liquid held the answers for the future. "I'd like to believe that our dreams eventually do come true. At least some version of them. The wisdom we gain over time has a way of altering our perspective of reality."

She waited for him to continue. When he didn't, she said, "Sounds to me like you're speaking from experience."

He nodded. "Take football for example. As a child, I dreamed of playing in the NFL. When I got to high school, I was happy just to get a starting position on the varsity team. By the time I got to college, football was something I played with my friends on warm autumn afternoons. I'm thankful to have survived with only two concussions and a broken collar bone. Somewhere along the way, reality set in and my goals changed." He appeared to be struck by a thought, and his face brightened. He pointed at Scottie. "You know what you need? You need a fresh start."

"I would love a fresh start, if only I could get the image of Brad and his girlthing out of my head. Maybe if she wasn't so pretty and her chest wasn't so large I wouldn't feel so bad about myself."

"Come now, Scottie. Contrary to the way most guys talk, a girl's boobs aren't everything." His eyes twinkled with mischief. "But tell me anyway. How big are we talking?"

"Big!" Scottie held her hands way out in front of her breasts.

"Here, I'll show you." She reached for her camera bag on the floor.

His jaw slackened as he stared at her camera. "Please don't tell me you took pictures of them."

"I'm a photojournalist. What else was I going to do?" She powered on the camera and handed it to Guy. "Now I have the evidence I need to get an uncontested divorce."

He scrolled through the pictures."She has an impressive set, no doubt about it. But she's not my type. All that caked-on makeup doesn't do anything for me." He arrived at the last picture, the one of Brad on the ground with his feet tangled up in the sheet. "This is a classic. It would serve your husband right if you blasted this pic all over social media." He handed the camera back to her.

"Ha. If only I wasn't such a nice person." She placed the camera back in the bag, and hung it on the back of her bar stool.

"So you're a photojournalist." He studied her closely, as though seeing her in a new light. "Do you write much, or is your focus mainly on the photographs?"

"I've done my share of writing, a few articles for the *Richmond Times Dispatch* but mostly pieces for online blogs and news services. I'm twenty hours into my masters in journalism at VCU. It's taking me forever, because I'm going part-time, but my goal is to one day work for Reuters. I want to travel the world and report on serious issues."

"Good for you." He held his glass up to hers. "Here's to the next Christiane Amanpour." They clinked, and then took sips of their drinks. "Do you get to see much action?"

She rolled her eyes. "I haven't seen much of anything lately. There was certainly nothing exciting at the Republican convention."

Guy considered this for a minute. "Yeah, I can see where

your shots would all be pretty much the same. Aside for the lack of excitement, what did you think of the convention?"

"It was all right, I guess. As far as political conventions go. I'm not much of a politico."

"Then why did you go?" Guy asked.

"Because I'm looking for my big break, like every other journalist, and the Republican convention was the place to be this week." She sat back in her chair and crossed her legs. "Well, let me clarify that. It's inaccurate for me to say I'm not interested in politics. I just don't particularly care for the politicians. Most politicians I know are self-serving, backstabbing egomaniacs. What about you? Why were you at the convention?"

He stared at her, his mouth agape. "Like I'm willing to admit to being a politician after that speech."

"Okay, so maybe my characterization was a bit harsh. I just wish the politicians would stop arguing and put their time to good use. If you ask me, the true heroes in this country are middle-class moms and dads making sacrifices to raise their children. And we can't forget about the men and women in the military. I take you for one of the good guys. Maybe Homeland Security or Secret Service."

An expression of disappointment or anger, a look Scottie couldn't interpret, crossed his face. "I sure as hell want to be considered one of the good guys," he mumbled.

"I'm sorry if I made you uncomfortable. I have a problem with impulse control. Feel free to put a clamp on my lips."

He drained the rest of his drink, and raised his empty glass at the bartender. "Let's order another drink and change the conversation. I'm declaring cheating husbands and politics off-limits."

"You're on," she said, and for the next hour, through two more drinks and a dozen oysters on the half shell, they talked about everything and nothing. She told him all about growing up on the farm and he, in turn, told her about his childhood living on a cattle ranch in Wyoming.

The more Guy drank, the more his right eyelid drooped, the slower he spoke, the rosier his adorable cheeks grew. His leg brushed against hers more than once, sending tingles down her spine. By the time the bartender made the last call, she was crushing on him hard. If not for her wounded heart, she would have dragged him to her room and torn his clothes off. Despite her drunken state, she knew she was too vulnerable, even for a rebound fling.

They paid the bill, splitting it between the two of them, and staggered out into the lobby, more than a little tipsy. They stopped in the middle of the atrium to admire the decorative ceiling and grand staircase.

"This hotel is seriously cool," Guy said.

"I agree. I'm so proud of Richmond's heritage. Did you know the Jefferson is on the National Register of Historic Places?" A lot of influential people have stayed here over the years."

"That doesn't surprise me."

"Hey!" A thought occurred to her and she play-punched him on the arm. "I hope you're not staying at the Jefferson on taxpayer dollars."

He furrowed his brow in confusion. "Taxpayer dollars?"

She placed her hands on her hips. "You work for the government, don't you?"

His face cleared. "Oh right, the government." He looped his arm through hers and dragged her over to the elevator. "Actually, the event director here is a friend of mine from college. She comped me a room." He held his finger to his lips. "But don't tell anyone."

"Lucky you." It irked her more than a little that he'd

probably flirted his way into free accommodations when she'd forked out three hundred dollars for a room the size of a closet.

Guy pressed the up button. When the elevator doors slid open, he held out his hand and smiled. "Can I offer you a ride?"

She giggled, thinking about the ride she'd like to take him on. And then she drew a straight face when the image of her husband in the bed with another woman popped into her head. She refused to stoop to Brad's level, even if her marriage was unofficially over.

"Sure," she said. "But only to my floor. No farther."

"Now it's you who can trust me. My intentions are strictly honorable."

Once they were alone in the elevator heading up to the third floor, she had to summon every bit of self-control not to wrap her arms around his neck and kiss him with every bit of pent-up passion she possessed. *Down, Scottie,* she said to herself. *This might seem like a good idea now, but you will hate yourself in the morning.*

"Why are you so convinced I work for the Secret Service?" he asked, breaking the awkward silence. "Do I look like a Secret Service agent?"

She closed her left eye, and studied him with her right. He definitely fit the bill in his gray suit with his military-style haircut. "Throw in some Ray-Ban sunglasses and an earpiece thingy, and I'd have to say, yeah, you do."

"Why not the CIA or the FBI?" he asked.

She contemplated the idea. "Mainly because I can't imagine either organization sending agents to the Republican convention. Unless..."—her eyebrows shot up—"you were on a secret mission."

The elevator doors opened onto her floor.

"That's it, isn't it?" Her eyes sparkled with excitement. "You were on a secret mission."

He chuckled, and then nudged her out of the elevator. "That's right, Scottie. A top-secret mission. If I told you about it, I'd have to kill you."

4

GUY LEFT RICHMOND before the sun came up the following morning, aiming to get to his office by eight. The storm system, after raining all night, had finally moved out of the area. But the highway remained slippery. His head throbbing, he gripped the steering wheel of his Ford rental car and drove as fast as he could. Thoughts of the early morning DC traffic he anticipated made his headache worse.

Scottie. What a fireball she turned out to be. It'd been years since he'd met anyone whose company he enjoyed as much as hers. He was as attracted to her physically as he was to her personality. He identified with her impulsive nature. He'd been like that once, before life had forced him into early adulthood. He admired Scottie for maintaining a positive attitude despite the mountain of shit she was dealing with. And she was definitely dealing with a mountain of shit. Which complicated the situation. He didn't think it wise for her to start a relationship so soon after the breakup of her marriage. Leave it to him to find the girl of his dreams, only to have her weigh in over the baggage limit.

The timing was all wrong for him as well. He could not afford the distraction at such a pivotal point in his career. He was at the top of his game. His performance during the next three months would determine what happened after the election. He needed to distance himself from Scottie. She posed way too much of a risk.

In the console beside him, his cell phone lit up with a Washington area code number he didn't recognize. He accepted the call. "Guy Jordan," he said, his voice froggy from too much whiskey.

"Good morning, Guy. This is Andrew Blackmore."

At the sound of his boss's voice, Guy sat up straighter in the driver's seat. Blackmore only called on rare occasions, with good news or bad news but never anything in between. "Morning, sir. I hope you are feeling well."

"As a matter of fact, I'm feeling exceptionally well after our performance in Cleveland," Blackmore said.

Guy imagined the toothy grin on his boss's lips. "Glad to hear it, sir. We're fortunate things went according to plan."

"They did indeed. Without a hitch. I'd like to meet with you, if you can spare me a few minutes around eight. I'm tied up in meetings for most of the day after that."

The hairs on the back of Guy's neck stood to attention. His mind raced. What could he possibly have done wrong in Cleveland? He coughed to clear his throat. "Actually, sir, I'm on my way back from Richmond. I was rerouted there last night because of the weather. I hope to make it to the office by eight, but that all depends on the traffic in Alexandria."

"Oh, right. Bad business that storm system. I'm glad you landed someplace safe."

"Can we meet sometime tomorrow?"

"That won't be necessary. I didn't have anything pressing I needed to talk to you about. I believe in offering praise when praise is due, and I wanted to congratulate you on a job well done in Cleveland. Keep it up, son, and I'll have a job for you on my team come January."

"Thank you, sir. I'd like that very much. Feel free to call me anytime I can be of assistance." Guy ended the call and wiped his sweaty hands on his pant legs.

His cell phone rang again almost immediately. This time the caller was his coworker Rich.

"Where are you, bro? The boss is in the house. He's handing out jobs like breath mints."

So Guy wasn't the only one receiving praise from the big man. "Tell me about it. I just hung up with him. He's in a good mood for sure. I'm on my way home from Virginia. I had to make an overnight detour because of the weather."

"Oh, that's right. I forgot you were booked on the earlier flight. All commercial flights were canceled from four o'clock on, including ours. Lucky us. We got to ride home on the Lear."

Guy's heart sank. He'd missed out on a chance to ride on Blackmore's private plane. "Yeah, lucky you."

"Anyway, we had an impromptu planning session with Blackmore on the way home. Get here as soon as you can. We have a lot of work to do."

Guy threw the phone on the floorboard of the passenger side. He shared the same job titles, the same responsibilities and duties, with Rich and James, but somehow they always managed to get one step ahead. They came from old-moneyed New England families. One graduated from Harvard, the other from Yale. If things didn't work out in November, their fathers had connections that would open doors for them at places considered off-limits to ranch hands from Wyoming.

Good thing he and Scottie never exchanged phone numbers. If the stars aligned and their paths crossed after the election, he would consider asking her out on a date. But for the next three months, his moment in the limelight, he needed to focus on his career, and network with anybody who might one day be of benefit to him.

5

SCOTTIE WOKE AROUND eleven with a dry mouth, an aching head, and a hole in her chest where her heart used to be. How could she possibly still have feelings for Brad? He'd broken all his promises to her, refused to support her when she needed him the most, and cheated on her with another woman.

Because, Scottie, your mind can't tell your heart how to love.

If only she could flip a switch and turn off her feelings.

Regret topped her list of emotions, followed closely by disappointment, frustration, and loneliness. She regretted all the hopes and dreams that would never come true. Regretted that she and Brad no longer brought out the best in one another. Regretted the three miscarriages. Regretted that she was now a thirty-year-old soon to be divorcée all alone in the world.

She texted her brother: *Are you swamped at work or do you have time for lunch?*

He texted back right away: *I'm starving. I'll meet you at the Urban Farmhouse Market in 45 mins.*

A converted historic warehouse, the Urban Farmhouse opened its oversized French doors on nice days, providing their patrons with a unique sidewalk cafe experience. Will was sipping iced tea and perusing the *Richmond Times Dispatch* at a curbside table when she arrived an hour later.

"How'd you score this table?" she asked, giving him a peck on the cheek when he stood to greet her.

He hooked a thumb at an attractive blonde waitress attending to customers at a table just inside the French doors. "She owes me a favor. I—"

"Please, spare me the details," she said, holding her palm out to shut him up.

He appeared wounded. "Why do you always assume the worst of me? For your information, I shared my Uber with her last weekend. She wanted to split the cost, but when I told her it wasn't necessary, she offered to seat me at the best table in the house the next time I came to the restaurant."

"Then I guess it's our lucky day." She dropped her bag on the table and collapsed in the chair opposite him.

The waitress rushed to their table with her pitcher of tea. "What can I get you?" she asked Scottie as she refilled Will's glass.

"Tea is fine," Scottie said.

"Liza, this is my sister, Scottie,"

Scottie shot her brother a look—*We wouldn't want Liza to think I'm your date, now would we?*—before offering the waitress a genuine smile. "Nice to meet you, Liza."

"Can we get a couple of menus too, please? When you get a chance, of course." Will licked his lips as he watched Liza's shapely rear end depart their table.

"Careful, bro, your tongue's hanging out."

He shifted back around to face Scottie. "Okay. What gives? Did you wake up on Brad's side of the bed this morning?"

"Ha-ha. As a matter of fact, I woke up at the Jefferson this morning." She removed her iPad from her bag, clicked on the pictures she'd downloaded from the night before, and slid it across the table to her brother.

Will's chocolate eyes bulged out of their sockets. "Nice rack."

Scottie glanced down at the woman sitting astride her husband. "Are you kidding me? Those are fake."

"Fake or not, I'd like to get my paws on those giant melons." He held his hands out in front of him as though massaging the woman's breasts.

Scottie smacked his hands away. She knew he was making light of the situation for her benefit, but she wasn't in the mood.

Propping his elbows on the table, he leaned in to get a closer look at Scottie's face. "Don't tell me you still have feelings for him?"

Her Ray-Ban sunglasses hid the tears, but her quivering chin gave her away.

"Come on, Scottie. After all he's done to you and now this?" He pointed at the iPad.

"I haven't been in love with him for some time, but I still care about him. I can't wave a wand and make those feelings magically disappear. Brad and I went through a lot together. I married him, Will. I made a commitment to him, and I'm sad we couldn't make that Happily Ever After work."

"I get your point." Will sat back in his chair and sipped his tea. "Why don't you try to think about it like this? You are finally free from the ball and chain you've been dragging around for years. You can do all those things you've been talking about doing. You can move to New York or DC and start a new life, focus on your career."

She'd been too blinded by the agony of Brad's betrayal to think much about the freedom a divorce would offer her. She'd grown tired of the limitations of freelance photojournalism, namely, the meager compensation for the hours she'd camped out in suspect places waiting for an opportunity that would make her career. She enjoyed the leisure side of her job, the side that paid the bills, shooting special events like weddings and selling her photographs to stock image websites such as Shutterstock. But that aspect of photography would never be anything more than a hobby. As a photojournalist, she'd developed not only her own personal style, edgy and fresh, but also a solid reputation with the big players, including the *Associated Press*. But lately, the drama in her personal life had kept her anchored to Richmond, shackled to her husband. With Brad out of her life, she could pursue her dream job with Reuters. She longed to travel overseas, to cover a different kind of story. She'd grown tired of mass shootings, police brutality, and bickering politicians. She wanted to report on worldwide affairs and issues that mattered to her, like disease and hunger and war.

She unfolded her napkin and dabbed at her tears. "It's not that easy," she said, sniffling.

"Like hell it's not. Look,"—he reached for her hand—"I get that you're afraid to move on. You were married to the guy for seven years. But it's okay to let go. Think about it. If you stay with Brad, he will continue to bring you down. And that is not who you are. Pick yourself up. Brush yourself off. And set yourself free."

Liza appeared at the table, interrupting Will's impassioned speech. She slid a glass of iced tea across the table to Scottie and dropped menus in front of each of them before heading on to another table. This time Will refrained from checking out her bottom.

Scottie stirred sweetener in her tea. "Do you really think I can do it, Will? Make it big as a photojournalist?"

"There's no doubt in my mind," he said without hesitation.

"Not only do you have the talent, you have the work ethic and drive to succeed."

Hope danced across Scottie's chest. She relished the idea of reclaiming her life.

While Will scanned the brunch specials on the menu, Scottie removed her phone from her bag and texted her husband: *Pack your bags and get out of my house.*

His response was instant: *I'm so sorry. I made a huge mistake. Please come home so we can talk about it.*

What home? You destroyed that. But the house belongs to me and I want you out of there today.

Her father, deeming the real estate a solid investment, had given Scottie the money for the down payment on their row house with the stipulation that the title be drawn up in her name alone. Brad had not contributed one penny toward the mortgage in the two years they'd lived there.

Her husband was a financial deadweight. Not having to make the minimum payment on his maxed-out credit cards alone would free up some much-needed cash.

Brad texted: *I don't have anywhere to go.*

Scottie: *What about the slut with the fake boobs you slept with in my bed? Go stay with her.*

Brad: *Don't be like this, Scottie. We can work through our problems.*

Scottie: *Get out, Brad!!!!!*

Brad: *Get a court order.*

"Ugh." She slammed the phone down on the table.

Will looked up from the menu. "What?"

She launched the phone across the table to him. Will read the texts and handed her back the phone. "Call Dad, Scottie. You're gonna need his team of attorneys."

"I can't drag Dad into my life again. I've already put him through so much."

Her father was the Westport in Westport and Johnson, Attorneys at Law, a full-service family practice offering legal counsel for anything from estate planning to capital murder. Back in December, when Scottie found herself in need of a criminal attorney, Len Bingham, one of her father's trusted partners, had offered a sympathetic ear and sound legal advice.

"Come on, sis. We're talking about Dad, here. He'd do anything for you. That's what dads are for."

Scottie set down her tea glass and moved to the edge of her seat, preparing to leave. "Nope. I'm going to have to figure this out myself."

At some point in time, she needed to grow up. And Scottie thought that time had come, with one failed marriage, three miscarriages, and a near brush with the law over a child abduction— no matter how innocent it was—under her belt.

Her brother's faced filled with concern. "What're you planning, Scott? The last thing you need is more trouble."

She picked up her bag and stood to leave. "Don't worry about it. I know what I'm doing."

She had no intention of approaching the situation unprepared. Ever since opening her eyes that morning, she'd been formulating her plan. She understood the stakes. One of her first priorities was to get her husband out of her house before he had a chance to pilfer her belongings. She owed Brad nothing, except maybe fifty percent of the wedding gifts. He could have the fine china, but the furniture was mostly hers, many of the pieces antiques she'd purchased with her own money and lovingly restored herself.

Will tugged at Scottie's arm, pulling her back down to her chair. "Why don't we order some food and talk this thing through?"

"I can't, Will." She popped back up. "If I'm going to be on my own, I need to learn how to fight my own battles. You can't always be my hero." She cupped his cheek in her hand. "But I love you for trying."

"But I've always been your hero," he said, looking up at her.

"I know that, and I truly appreciate it, and all your love and concern. But this time is different."

He stood to face her. "Will you promise to call me if you need me?"

"I'll always need you, little brother. I need you to make me laugh, and to run interference in my arguments with Mom. What *you* don't need is *me* constantly dragging you into my shit-storms. I can be strong when I need to be. And I need to be strong now. I need to face Brad alone."

"You're stronger than a herd of elephants, Scott. You've just been hiding from yourself for the past few years, afraid to come out for fear of getting hurt. And with good reason. You've been through a lot. But that's all behind you now." He spun her around and gave her a gentle shove as he whispered, "Be free, little birdie. Spread your wings and fly."

6

THE ATTENDANT AT Grove Avenue Exxon located the nail, plugged the hole, and remounted Scottie's tire in less than thirty minutes. She stopped at Elwood Thompson for a Mean Green smoothie before heading back to the Fan.

She parked a block away from her house. While waiting for Brad to leave for work, she worked her way down the list of locksmiths that Siri provided until she found one with a reasonable quote who could get the job done that day. At ten minutes before three, as she'd predicted, the front door opened and Brad hustled down the steps to his Tahoe. She waited a few more minutes, in case he returned for something he'd forgotten, and then moved the Mini to the front of her house.

Built in 1910, her row house offered stunning architectural details—ten-foot ceilings, intricately carved woodworking, and interior French doors separating the formal rooms. An eclectic mix of antique furniture and contemporary art accented the subtle tones on the walls. Scottie had chosen each piece with careful consideration, her flawless taste apparent throughout. Nothing in the house represented Brad's personality with the exception of the empty beer cans and overflowing ashtrays scattered about. In recent years, he had regressed to his teenage days, throwing wild parties as soon as the adult left town. Sadly, the adult in this case was his wife, and his punishment for bad behavior was divorce.

Scottie started upstairs in the master bedroom and worked her way down. She stripped the bed of the tangled linens, balled them up, and tossed them down the stairs. She remade the bed with clean sheets and pillowcases—the lavender 500-count set that matched the walls, the ones Brad said made him have homosexual dreams. She emptied the dresser drawers and closet of her husband's clothes, and placed them in boxes she brought down from the attic. She packed his toiletries in his dopp kit and stuffed it, along with the contents of his bedside table, in a duffel bag. Once the boxes were neatly stacked in the foyer beside the front door, she collected all the trash from downstairs in a large Hefty bag. She tossed out the leftover cartons of Chinese food and Styrofoam takeout containers, vowing to allow only healthy food in her refrigerator from now on.

She Windexed and Pledged the tops of the counters and furniture, wiping away the sticky remnants of Brad's three-day bender. She was vacuuming the sisal rugs when the locksmith arrived. She'd been so anxious to get her locks changed, she hadn't taken the time to read the online reviews or consider why J. W. Locksmith was the cheapest. The leathery skin on Johnny White's face spoke of too much time on the beach smoking cigarettes.

"You moving out?" Johnny asked when he saw the boxes stacked beside the front door. Licking his lips, his eyes traveled her body before landing on her chest.

"Actually, I'm moving in." She didn't want to give the creep the impression that she lived alone. "I want you to change the locks on the knobs and the dead bolts on this door. If you will just follow me, I have another one to show you." She felt his beady eyes on her butt when he walked behind her to the family room. "The one back here," she said as she unlocked the French door that led to her courtyard.

When he was still working at dinnertime, she berated herself for not asking for a job estimate instead of agreeing to the hourly rate. What should have taken less than an hour took Johnny almost three. When he finally left a few minutes before seven, she was famished and more than a little irritated by his bad jokes and suggestive innuendo.

She was finishing the last bite of her BLT when Will called. "Have you talked to Brad yet?"

"No. He's still at work."

"Did you call Dad like I suggested?"

"I'm not going to drag Dad into this," Scottie said. "I told you that earlier. I can handle Brad myself."

"I have a bad feeling about this, Scot. I don't think you should confront Brad by yourself."

"I'm not planning to confront him. I had the locks changed."

"I'm coming over," Will said without hesitation.

"No, you're not. I appreciate your concern, little brother, but I got this."

"Seriously, Scottie. Think about what you're doing here. When Brad realizes you've locked him out, he'll go postal."

"He can't hurt me if he can't get in." She walked her empty plate to the sink. "I'll be fine. Truly. Don't you have big party plans for your Friday night? Go out and have fun and stop worrying about me." She ended the call before he could respond.

She leaned back against the counter and finished her glass of sweet tea. Since she'd opened her eyes that morning, she'd been a woman on a mission, a scorned wife out for blood. Will was right—she hadn't stopped long enough to think about what her husband might do when he realized she'd kicked him out of the house. Story of her life—instead of making a level-headed plan, she'd reacted to her emotions. She was an easy target, alone in her house with nothing to protect her except a brand-new set of Schlage locks. Not that Brad had ever been abusive toward her. But he'd shown his nasty temper a time or two in situations not nearly as confrontational as her locking him out of the house and leaving all his earthly goods on the sidewalk out front.

To make matters worse, after her near brush with the law at Christmas, she couldn't call the police if she needed them.

She waited until nightfall before moving the boxes of his belongings to the sidewalk in front of her house. She poured herself a glass of milk, triple-checked the locks on the windows and doors, and then trudged up the stairs to the nursery. She went to the crib and ran her hand across the soft cotton sheet. She imagined baby Mary sleeping soundly on her tummy, her tiny hands folded beneath her cheek. This room held too many painful memories for Scottie—three miscarriages, one of them late term, and Mary. It was clear now, she was never meant to have Brad's baby. Maybe one day she'd become a mother, but for the immediate future, for the sake of her wounded soul, she needed to focus her attention on her career. For her own peace of mind, she would donate the contents of her nursery to charity and turn the room into a study.

She closed the nursery door, and went down the hall to the master bedroom. She removed six poster-size framed photographs from the back of her closet, and spread them out on her king-size bed. She studied the pained expressions of the homeless friends she'd met in Monroe Park, the Five as she'd come to know them. With plans for a gallery showing in New York, she'd worked on this series for nearly a year. But that was before Mary.

She'd long since destroyed the digital files on her hard drive, but she'd kept the framed photographs in the hopes of one day returning them to their place on the wall in her family room. She understood now that rehanging them would never be a safe choice. One by one, she turned the frames face down on the bed, ripped off the paper backings, and removed the photographs. She found a pair of scissors in her bedside table drawer and shredded the photographs into tiny little pieces, destroying the last remaining physical evidence that linked her to the Missing Baby Case of Monroe Park.

Sweeping the shredded photographs into the bathroom wastebasket, she carried the trashcan downstairs and dumped it into the fireplace in the family room. She lit a long wooden match and set fire to a year's worth of meticulous work.

Back upstairs, she changed into yoga pants and a long-sleeved T-shirt and crawled into bed to await her husband's return. Unable to sleep, she downloaded the second in the *Game of Thrones* series and read until the pounding of the brass knocker and ringing of the bell startled her a few minutes past midnight. Removing her phone from the bedside table, she rolled off the bed and crawled to the window. Standing flush against the wall, out of the way of the window, she watched her husband throw an adult-sized temper tantrum on the lawn below. He kicked at the boxes of his belongings while screaming insults too nasty to repeat into the silent night. The Yorkie Terrors in the backyard next door sprang into action, alerting the neighbors to danger with their excessive barking. Lights flashed on up and down the street, while the silhouette of Mrs. Lucas's hunched-over body appeared in the upstairs window of the house across from them.

When a yellow Volkswagen Beetle pulled alongside the curb, interrupting his tantrum, Brad stomped over to speak to the driver. Peering through the blinds, Scottie caught a glimpse of the driver's long dark hair as she leaned across the front seat to get a better view of the chaos in the front yard. Brad bent down behind the Beetle to talk to the driver. A minute later, the

Volkswagen sped away, leaving Brad in the middle of the street with a twelve-pack of beer tucked under his arm.

He set the twelve-pack down on the sidewalk and removed his cell phone from his pocket. Scottie's phone vibrated in her hand with a stream of texts from her husband, pleading with her to let him in so they could talk, claiming he had nowhere to go and no money to pay for a hotel room. When she didn't respond, Brad tore open the twelve-pack and pitched a bottle of beer at the house. Scottie, watching in horror, could see the whites of his eyes and teeth as his face lit up with amusement. He bombarded the house, heaving bottle after bottle against the brick, the sound of shattering glass resonating throughout the block.

Scottie slid down the wall to the floor, terrified, uncertain what to do. She was too concerned they might somehow connect her to the Missing Baby Case to call the police. Her parents lived too far away to be of any use. She couldn't very well ask her brother for help, after she'd been so insistent on handling the situation herself. Which left her no choice but to wait it out.

She was relieved to hear her next-door neighbor call across the yard, "Brad, is that you? What's going on out there?"

"Mind your own damn business, Chuck," Brad shouted back.

"I can't very well do that with you hurling beer bottles at your house like a madman. Is Scottie inside? Did the two of you have some kind of fight?"

Another bottle exploded against the house.

"I'm warning you, Brad. If you do it again, I'm going to call the police."

Scottie sucked in her breath. She wanted the assault on her house to end, but not if it meant calling in the police. Although she'd destroyed the last of the physical evidence, Brad knew enough about her involvement in the Missing Baby Case to rat her out if he got mad enough. And he certainly appeared to be mad enough.

Scottie heard her husband's deflated voice. "Don't call the police, Chuck. I'm sorry, man. I'm leaving. I just need a minute to get my things together."

Peeking over the windowsill, she watched Brad gather his belongings and load the boxes in the back of his Tahoe. He removed the two remaining unopened bottles of beer from the twelve-pack and stuffed them in his pockets. After climbing into the driver's side, he peeled away from the curb and disappeared into the dark night.

Scottie dove onto the bed and buried her face in her pillow. How had things spiraled so far out of control? When she graduated from the University of Virginia eight years ago, her life had been mapped out in a straight and narrow path in front of her. The plan was for her to support Brad, freelancing as a photojournalist while he attended medical school. Somewhere along that path, Brad's ambition had gone south and Scottie had gotten lost in her hormonal yearnings to have a baby.

7

SCOTTIE TOSSED AND turned for most of the night, imagining noises and dreaming of strange men throwing Molotov cocktails made out of Budweiser bottles at her home. Although common sense told her Brad would not come back that night, it was no match for her overactive imagination and her fragile state of mind. Huddled under the covers, a complete emotional wreck, she thought of her earlier conversation with Will. Again, he had been right. She would seek her parents' help—and the sooner the better.

When Scottie arrived at her family's farm a few minutes after eight the following morning, she found her father on the terrace, off the kitchen, eating breakfast—the usual poached egg on wheat toast he'd eaten every day since she was a little girl.

"Hello, honey. What a pleasant surprise." He rose out of his chair to greet her. Kissing her cheek, he asked, "Can I offer you some breakfast?"

"No, but thanks. I ate a bowl of cereal before I left home, and stopped at Starbucks on the way out." She held up her paper coffee cup.

"Then have a seat and tell me about your trip. I want to hear all about the convention."

Scottie hung her bag over the back of the wrought iron chair and lowered herself to the seat next to him. "The convention was predictable but inspiring, like a pep rally for the Dallas Cowboys' season opener. I don't understand why the political parties spend so much money on an event that serves little purpose."

"Nor do I. The process has changed a great deal since I was your age. Back then, the primary focus of the convention was nominating the candidate out of more than one hopeful." He pointed his fork at her. "But the photographs you sold to the *Associated Press* were some of your best work."

"Thanks, Dad. I'm not sure I agree with you, but I appreciate the vote of confidence. Lucky me, I get to do it all over again in three days."

"Ah, but don't forget about your trip to Rio, the light at the end of your tunnel."

The reminder of her upcoming trip brought a smile to her face. "That's true. I am excited about going to the Olympics."

Her father forked off a bite of toast and dragged it through the yolk before popping it in his mouth. "As much as I hate the idea of you traveling to Brazil alone."

"I'll be fine. It's my job. You've got to stop worrying about me." The words escaped her mouth before she had a chance to think about them. Her father would worry even more once she told him about the breakup of her marriage and Brad's assault on the house.

Shielding her eyes from the sun, Scottie peered through the French doors into the kitchen. "Where's Mom?"

He motioned toward their second-floor bedroom. "Getting her beauty sleep. Where else on a Saturday morning?"

"Yes, of course. Mommy's time." Scottie chuckled.

He popped a vitamin into his mouth and swallowed it down

with juice. "She got up early during the week, but she made sure we all knew her sleeping-in time on weekends was sacred."

"Actually, Dad, Will and I looked forward to it because you always used that time to do something special with us." She smiled as memories of Saturday mornings flashed through her mind—the three of them taking horseback rides in warmer months on trails surrounding their farm, and in winter months enjoying brunch at the Red Barn Cafe in Centerville.

"I'm sure you didn't drive all the way out here to discuss the convention or reminisce. What's on your mind, Scottie?" Stuart asked.

Barbara's absence served Scottie well today. While they argued with one another over the small stuff, like whether to eat Mexican food or Italian, her parents typically agreed on the big picture issues. Breaking the news to her father first would give her a chance to test the waters for their reaction to her separation from Brad. While they'd never approved of her husband, they believed wholeheartedly in the sanctity of marriage. "Marriage is hard work," she'd heard her mother say more than once. "I've seen so many couples call it quits too easily. You must have a fair balance of give and take to succeed."

"You know me so well, Daddy." She paused, gathering her nerve. "There's really no easy way to say this, except to come out and say it. I need to hire one of your attorneys. One who specializes in divorce, that is."

Her father stopped chewing, but his expression remained impassive. Scottie had often wondered if Poker Face 101 was a requisite course in law school—*How to keep a blank face when your client confesses his crimes.*

"I'm sorry, sweetheart. My feelings for Brad aside, I hate to see you hurt."

"I appreciate that, Dad. It's not easy, but I know it's for the best."

Stuart pushed his plate away, abandoning his egg, and sat back in his chair. "Do you want to tell me what happened?"

"I caught him in bed with another woman." She removed her iPad from her bag and set it on the table. "I took some photographs, if you want to see them."

Stuart glanced down at the iPad, then back up at her. "I'd rather you save them for the attorney. That's too much information for me, as you youngsters like to say. When did this happen?"

"On Thursday night, when I got home from Cleveland."

Scottie recounted the events of the past thirty-six hours. She told him about spending the night at the Jefferson and changing the locks on the doors, including Brad's subsequent assault with beer bottles on her house.

"What a mess. Was there a lot of glass?"

"You have no idea, but I cleaned most of it up this morning. At least the pieces I could see. I hope some neighborhood kid doesn't cut his foot running through our yard."

"Why didn't you call me? I would've been there right away."

Scottie had a mental image of her father arriving on the scene with an arsenal of weapons in the back of his ancient Jeep Wagoneer. "I didn't want to drag you into my problems again, after what happened at Christmas."

"That's what your mother and I are here for, honey. You can come to us with your problems anytime, day or night. I thought you knew that."

She nodded, not trusting herself to speak.

"You deserve so much more than he's capable of offering you."

Whether or not her husband had ever been capable of providing the life he'd promised her, lately he'd been unwilling to even try. "Brad is not the same man I met in college. I know you and Mom never saw his true potential. Believe me, he's plenty smart. Unfortunately he lacks the work ethic to put that intelligence to use."

"People change, sweetheart, and not always for the better."

Scottie gnawed on her lower lip. "Our marriage hasn't worked for some time. I've just been too stubborn to admit it, even to myself."

Stuart winked at her. "You inherited that trait from your mother."

Scottie smiled. "That's not true and you know it." She was every bit her father's daughter, especially when it came to his fiery disposition.

"After the way Brad lost his temper last night, I'm scared to be alone in my house," she said. "Can I stay here for a few days?"

"Stay as long as you'd like. I'll call Gloria Simpson this afternoon and put her on alert. She's one of the best, as far as divorce attorneys go."

"Thank you. I'll feel more comfortable confiding in a female."

"We'll get a restraining order if we have to," Stuart said. "Your name is the only one on the deed, so technically he has no claim to the property."

"What if he sues for alimony?" Scottie asked.

"Let's take it one step at a time. Hopefully it won't come to that."

*

Scottie was stretched out on her bed, reading through her notes from the convention, when her mother sought her out a little while later.

"There you are, sweetheart. I've been looking all over for

you." She sat down on the side of the bed. "Your father thought you'd gone down to the stables."

"I've been getting acquainted with my new room," she said, looking around at her mother's recent renovations to her childhood bedroom. "I feel like I'm floating on a cloud in the midst of all this white." Aside from the four-poster mahogany bed and antique chest of drawers, all the accoutrements were white—fabrics, carpet, and wall color.

"I'm glad you like it, although I'm sorry your visit is under such difficult circumstances."

"So Dad told you." Scottie wasn't sure he would, but she was glad he had.

"He didn't want you to have to repeat the story again." Barbara placed her hand on the bed, absentmindedly smoothing out the coverlet. "I want you to know you have my full support. We'll have you back on your feet in no time. You'll meet someone new, and have all the babies you've ever wanted."

"If only I *could* divorce my fertility problems."

"Things usually work out the way they were meant to be. Once you meet the right man, everything else will fall into place. I believe it in my heart."

Scottie admired her mother's eternal optimism. "I hope you're right, Mom." In Barbara's mind, dreams came true, simply because she believed in them.

"Your father is planning a family cookout in honor of your visit. Will is on his way out. We thought we'd spend the afternoon by the pool, then shoot skeet later if it's not too hot."

"Can we please do it another time?" Scottie sank deeper into the pillows. "I'd rather stay nestled up in all these fluffy linens. Besides, I'm not in the mood to listen to Will tell me I told you so about what happened last night."

"He won't say a word. Your father has already talked to him

about it." Barbara slid off the bed and pulled Scottie to her feet. "Change into your bathing suit and meet me at the pool. Your father has gone to the store for supplies and Will should be here any minute."

As it turned out, a relaxing afternoon by the pool with her family was exactly what Scottie needed. Stretched out in the shade on a lounge chair, Barbara read the latest Elin Hildebrand novel while Scottie played Marco Polo and underwater tag with her father and Will. Despite his quadruple bypass eighteen months earlier, or perhaps because of it, her father appeared to be in excellent shape. He'd always been full of energy, but in the years prior to his heart attack, he had slowed down and put on weight. It tickled Scottie to see him acting like a forty-year-old man again.

When the heat of the afternoon became too much to bear, instead of shooting skeet, Will and Stuart barbecued ribs in the Big Green Egg while Barbara and Scottie sipped mojitos in the rocking chairs on the back porch. It was nearly eight o'clock before they got around to eating.

Once they were seated at the table on the terrace, Stuart said, "Before we dig into this delicious dinner, I'd like to propose a toast." He popped the cork on a bottle of Vueve Clicquot champagne, and poured four glasses.

"What's the occasion?" Will asked, as Stuart handed each of them a glass.

"We are toasting my beautiful bride." His face full of love, he held his glass up to Barbara.

"I totally forgot! Your anniversary," Scottie said as she clicked glasses with her parents and brother. "It's not today, is it?"

"No, it's Monday, the twenty-fifth." Barbara said, her cheeks rosy with happiness. "This is a big one for us, you know."

"Thirty-five years," Stuart said, his face beaming with pride. "I'm taking your mother on an Alaskan cruise to celebrate."

"Wow. Thirty-five years certainly calls for a celebration." Scottie admired her parents. Surviving the ups and downs of marriage for more than three decades was definitely something to brag about. She questioned whether she could last in a relationship with anyone for that long, even a man who combined the looks of Channing Tatum with the personality of Prince Charming.

"When do you leave for your cruise?" Will asked.

"A week from Tuesday," Barbara answered.

"I'm feeling a little left out that you didn't invite Scottie and me," Will said, thrusting his lower lip forward.

"That would have made it a family vacation, not a second honeymoon." Stuart winked at his son. "Time for you to find your own bride."

Will rolled his eyes. "Here we go again."

"You're not getting any younger, you know," Barbara said.

Will puffed out his chest. "I can't help that I'm selective about who I go out with."

Champagne bubbles flew up Scottie's nose as she burst into laughter. "I've met some of the girls you go out with. I wouldn't exactly call them the marrying type."

"You know," Barbara said, clasping her hands together. "I think my friend Clara's daughter is moving back to Richmond from somewhere up north. If I remember correctly, she's unmarried. I know she's a doctor. A cardiologist, I believe." She picked her phone up off the table. "I'll text her and find out."

"Don't you dare." Will tried to grab the phone, but Barbara held it out of her son's reach.

Scottie slapped her brother on the shoulder. "I hate to say it, bro, but I agree with Mom and Dad. It's time for you to settle down. I'm so far ahead of you, it isn't funny. I've already been through one husband, and you can't even find a steady girlfriend."

Barbara finished her text and set her phone down on the table. "Having a cardiologist in the family might come in handy one day, especially when your father has another heart attack from eating all those ribs."

Three sets of eyes zeroed in on Stuart's plate, which was piled high with barbecue ribs. He grinned and licked the sauce off his lips.

"Seriously, Dad, should you be eating ribs?" Will asked.

"I'll have you know I've lost twenty pounds." Stuart sat up straighter in his chair and sucked in his gut. "I'm gluten free, fat free, and sugar free. Eating a rack of spare ribs once in a blue moon isn't going to kill me." He bit into another rib. "And if it does, I'll die a happy man."

They were all sharing a laugh when, out of the corner of her eye, Scottie glimpsed movement in the hydrangea bushes beside the pool. She grew still, the hairs on the back of her neck standing to attention.

Recognizing her daughter's concern, Barbara said, "Honey, is something wrong?"

Scottie kept her eye on the bushes for another minute or so. When the bushes remained still, she shook off the unnerving feeling that someone was watching them. "I guess I'm still a little unglued by everything that happened last night. For a moment there, I thought I saw someone hiding in the bushes."

8

AFTER POLISHING OFF another bottle of champagne and several after dinner drinks on the porch, Will opted to spend the night at the farm instead of paying Uber to drive him back to town. Scottie woke her brother early on Sunday, and together they cooked up an elaborate breakfast to celebrate their parents' anniversary, complete with french toast, sausage, and fresh roses cut from the garden.

Around noon, when Will left, Scottie grabbed her electronic devices and headed for the shade of the massive white oak at the edge of the lawn. The property sloped downhill from there and gave a view of the horse pastures. As a child, she'd spent many afternoons in the rope swing dreaming of becoming the first female president of the United States. And now, this week, when the Democratic Party nominated Senator Catherine Caine as the first female candidate for president, Scottie would be there to cover the event.

She spread an old quilt beneath the tree, and stretched out on her belly with her iPad. She was close enough to the house to connect to the Wifi, but far enough away from her parents' constant hovering. She appreciated their concern, but their lavish attention was grating on her nerves.

She scrolled through the articles she'd recently added to her reading list. In order to attract the attention of the decision-makers at Reuters, she would need to take her work to a new level. And the only way she knew to do that at a political convention was to offer a unique perspective on the candidate—a real challenge in this instance, considering the fifty-eight-year-old Massachusetts senator's pristine reputation and accomplished résumé. Catherine Caine's academic pursuits as an undergrad at Exeter and a law school student at Harvard were exemplary, as was her reputation in the Senate.

Every news agency and journalist in the country had scrutinized her background time and again. She'd never smoked pot in college, or sent classified emails from her personal server while holding a government office. There were no ghosts living in Caine's closet, only her immaculately tailored suits and Italian leather pumps. She and her husband presented a happy and united front, no evidence of any scandals afoot. Her three sons likewise enjoyed successful careers and had married role-model women.

As predicted, none of the articles on her reading list revealed anything Scottie didn't already know about the senator, or raise questions as to her integrity. The best she could hope for from the convention was a rare slip-up made by the candidate, an unflattering smirk or an offhanded comment.

Tired of lying on her stomach, Scottie sat back against the tree and opened her laptop. She launched Lightroom and began editing her photographs from last week's convention. Many of them held promise for generating a profit online.

So engrossed in her work, she didn't hear Brad approach until he was looming over her. "All work and no play makes Scottie a dull girl."

She slammed the laptop shut and scrambled to her feet.

"What do you want, Brad? I'm not alone, you know. My parents are inside." She glanced up at the house, disappointed to see that her father, who had been standing at the family-room window for the past hour, had disappeared.

"Just calm down. I didn't come here to hurt you. I just want to talk."

She took a step back, away from him. "That was you last night, wasn't it? Hiding in the bushes and spying on us while we ate."

"I wasn't spying on you, for crying out loud. I was hoping for a chance to talk to you alone. But that little douche-bag brother of yours has apparently appointed himself your bodyguard."

"Get off my property, Brad." She pointed at his Tahoe in the driveway. "There's nothing left to say. Our attorneys will do all the talking from now on."

"Come on, baby." He grabbed her wrist, but she jerked her hand away and started walking toward the house. "Don't be like this." He fell in step with her. "I made a mistake. It's nothing we can't work through."

"You slept with another woman in *our* bed, Brad. I could never get past that, even if I wanted to."

"Look." He took her by the arm and spun her around. "I understand you're upset, and you have every right to be, but just give me a chance to explain how I feel. We used to be so good together. We could have that relationship again."

While his remorse seemed genuine, she cautioned herself about falling into his trap again. "The sooner you realize our marriage is over, the sooner we can both move on."

"Baby, please." He wrapped his arm around her waist, trying to pull her in for a hug, but she pushed him away.

"Take your hands off my daughter!"

Hearing her father's voice, stern but calm, she stole a quick glance behind her, where she saw him standing on the terrace with his rifle trained on Brad's chest.

Removing his sunglasses, Brad squinted his bloodshot eyes at her father. "No need for weapons, Stuart. We're all friends here."

"That's funny. Being on the receiving end of beer bottle grenades sure as hell didn't feel very friendly to me," Scottie said to her husband, then turned to her father. "Put the rifle away, Daddy."

"I'm sorry about the other night, babe. I didn't mean for things to get so out of control." When Brad reached for her again, Stuart fired a shot in the air above his head. Ducking, Brad covered his head with his hands. "Jesus Christ, Stuart! Are you crazy?"

Scottie almost felt sorry for her husband. Almost. "Seriously, Dad. You're not helping the situation. Put the gun away! Brad just wants to talk for a minute. Then he's leaving."

Stuart aimed the rifle at Brad's car in the driveway and shot out the taillight. "You hurt my daughter, and I'll put the next bullet in your head. There's nothing left for you here, son. The sooner you realize that, the better off you'll be."

Mouth agape, Brad stared at his shattered taillight. "I have no intention of hurting her, Stuart. All I'm asking for is a chance to talk to her in private." When Stuart appeared skeptical, Brad added, "Just for a minute, sir."

"Fine, but I'm staying right here." Stuart retired the gun to the crook of his arm with the barrel aimed at the sky, standing guard like a sentinel.

Scottie turned to Brad. "He's right, you know. There is nothing left for you here."

Brad dropped to the ground next to the nearest tree. "I tried, Scottie. I really tried. For the sake of the babies as much as for you. Truth is, I haven't felt like myself in a really long time. Like I'm living someone else's life."

She sat down beside him. "We've both changed, Brad. It happens. It's no one's fault." She noticed for the first time the traces of white powder under his nose, the telltale sign of her husband's most recent bad habit. Which explained a lot about his volatile behavior of late—hurling bottles at the house and hiding out in her parents' shrubbery. All the more reason to keep him on a short leash. Setting him off could bring harm to her family or herself. And arguing with him might provoke him into going to the police with his knowledge of the Missing Baby Case. For all she knew, the police had filed their investigation away in a folder of unsolvable cases, but she couldn't afford to take that risk.

"Your parents warned us against getting married so young," he said. "Maybe we should have listened to them."

"No doubt Mom and Dad are the experts on marriage. They're celebrating their thirty-fifth anniversary this week, if you can believe that."

"That's impressive," he said, and she could tell he meant it.

"I don't regret our time together, Brad. I hope you understand that. I learned a lot about myself. I see the world through a different set of eyes because of our experiences."

"What will you do now?" he asked. "Will you stay in Richmond?"

"For as long as it takes Reuters to hire me."

He chucked her chin. "Photographing the world was always your dream. Before you let your obsession with having children get in the way."

She cocked her head to one side. *Obsessed?* Had she really been that consumed with having a baby?

"I still want a family, but now is not my time," she admitted.

"I wanted children," Brad said, "because I saw how much you wanted children. But I'm not sure I'm cut out to be a father."

"You will make a great father," she said. "One day. But first you need to stop snorting your paycheck up your nose, and figure out how to support a family."

His body grew rigid. "You knew?"

She shrugged. "I suspected. I'm an investigative reporter. Not much gets past me."

His eyebrows shot up.

She smiled. "Okay, so maybe a lot gets past me sometimes. But trust me, I noticed when you didn't contribute a nickel of your income to our household expenses. You need to get some help, Brad. Before you get in over your head. If you're not already in over your head."

He avoided her gaze. "Brandi, the girl from the other night, she's letting me stay with her as long as I don't do drugs."

WTF? she thought. *Ten minutes ago, he was begging for a reconciliation, and now he is practically admitting to being in a relationship with Brandi. He isn't sad about the breakup of his marriage. He is upset over losing his Sugar Mama.*

"In that case, you'd better wipe your nose before you go home." Scottie got to her feet. "Now, if you don't mind, I have a lot of work to do."

"I understand." He stood and kissed her cheek. "I'm glad we had a chance to talk."

"I wish you well, Brad." She stood glued to her spot under the tree and watched her husband round the corner of the house to the driveway, walking out of her life for good after eight long years.

Scottie joined her father on the terrace. "Seriously, Dad, was the gun really necessary?"

"Damn right," Stuart said. "After he went ballistic on you the other night, someone needed to set him straight."

"He's far from straight." Scottie watched Brad's Tahoe leave the driveway. "But I'm relieved that he's somebody else's problem now."

9

SCOTTIE SPENT THE rest of the day on Sunday in the family room watching the post-Republican and pre-Democratic convention coverage on the twenty-four-hour news networks. She could hardly wait until the end of the election, when the spotlight on the candidates and poll statistics no longer dominated the news.

Early in the afternoon on Monday, she drove downtown to her father's offices to meet with Gloria Simpson. Scottie found her no-nonsense approach and snarky disposition appropriate for a divorce attorney. She had no doubt Gloria could deliver a go–to-hell message with a smile when warranted.

"You've protected your assets well," Gloria said, pleased to see the deed to Scottie's house was in her name alone. "Obviously, custody won't be an issue. As far as alimony is concerned, if what you tell me is true, Brad earns enough on his own to support himself. We are in a good position to proceed."

With her safety no longer a concern, after the meeting, Scottie moved back into her house on West Avenue. She needed time to pay bills and do laundry and pack for her trip to Philadelphia.

She'd jumped at the opportunity when a friend offered her

condo in the historic district of downtown Philadelphia for the week of the Democratic convention. "You can stay all week if you'd like," Amy had suggested.

Imagining the money she could save on hotel expenses, Scottie said, "I'm tempted, but I hate to inconvenience you by running you out of your own home."

"Pu-lease. I won't even be here," Amy said. "I'm going with a group of friends to Rehoboth Beach. Only politicos are staying in town during the convention."

The four-hour drive to Philadelphia seemed like eight. After dropping her things at Amy's condo, Scottie changed into her running clothes and went for a power walk through historic Old City. She wished she had more time to explore the museums, old churches, and historical monuments. She spent Tuesday afternoon wandering around the Liberty Center, familiarizing herself with the space. She shot more than a thousand images during the first twenty-four hours, capturing the animated faces of politicians, speakers, and Democratic Party leaders. She took photographs of flags and banners and the crowd at large—plenty of material to sell online to patriotic Americans looking for any and everything washed in red, white, and blue. Unfortunately, not even one of her photos would be of interest to the news services. The one special moment she needed to make her career—the unique photograph that stood out from all the rest—had yet to present itself.

On Wednesday night, she was standing in line at concessions when she spotted Guy across the lobby deep in conversation with a strictly business-looking woman—a congresswoman if Scottie had to guess. Her stomach flip-flopped at the sight of his handsome face and muscular body in a dark-blue suit and red-striped tie. He didn't appear to see her at first. When another minute passed and he still didn't notice her, she began to wonder if he was ignoring her on purpose. The end of their night together at the Jefferson remained somewhat of a blur. *Did I do something to offend him?* she wondered.

She continued to watch him as discreetly as possible while she moved forward in the concession line. He eventually looked her way, and their eyes met. Scottie waved. He smiled back, but he took his time ending his conversation and making his way through the crowd to her side.

Guy leaned down and kissed her cheek. "It's nice to see you, Scottie." He eyed her camera. "Are you getting some good shots?"

"Nothing out of the ordinary. My images are about as uninspired as the photographer."

The woman in front of Scottie stepped away, clearing a space at the concession stand. "Would you like something?" she asked Guy.

His gaze bounced back and forth between the overhead menu and Scottie, as though he was struggling to make a decision. "You know what. I've been at this convention center all day, and I could use a real drink right about now. Care to join me?"

Scottie hesitated. "I'd hate to miss Byron Caine's speech." She wanted nothing more than to leave the crowded Liberty Center and go to a quiet spot with this attractive man whose smoky gray eyes turned her insides out, but she didn't want to appear overeager. She'd been out of the dating game for so long. Did women still play hard to get?

"I'm sure we can find a bar with a television," Guy said.

The impatient concessions worker tapped the counter. "What's it gonna be, lady?"

"I've changed my mind. I don't want anything after all," Scottie said, and stepped away from the counter.

Guy took her by the elbow and led her to the nearest entrance door.

"I'm blaming you if I miss my big break," Scottie said.

"I hardly think Byron Caine is going to reveal any deep dark secrets about his wife." He held the door open for her. "Where are you staying?"

"In a friend's condo off South Broad near Washington. What about you?"

"Farther north near Rittenhouse Square. Why don't we go somewhere near your place, and I'll catch a taxi back to my hotel from there?"

They took the Broad Street Line to the Ellsworth-Federal Station, then walked two blocks north to the first bar they came to, a pub specializing in local craft beers. The restaurant was crowded, but a table opened up by the window a few minutes after they arrived. The waitress seated them at the table, handed them menus, and recited a list of craft beers in a West Virginian mountain accent. They ordered a pitcher of Yards Philadelphia Pale Ale. As they waited for the waitress to return, they watched Byron Caine address the nation in closed caption on the big screen television behind the bar.

The pitcher arrived and Guy filled two frosty mugs. "So..." He handed a mug to Scottie. "I trust you sorted things out?"

"Depends on your definition of sorting things out. We made peace. We're leaving the rest to the divorce attorneys."

Scottie watched Guy's face for his reaction. Aside from a hint of a smile tugging at his lips, his expression remained impassive. "Normally I would say I'm sorry, but after what he did to you, I think you're much better off without him." Guy sipped his beer, and then licked the froth off his upper lip. "Is he the reason for your inspiration crisis?"

Scottie slunk back against the wooden bench seat. "Not in so many words. For the most part, I'm ecstatic over getting my life back. Problem is, now that I'm finally free to pursue my career, I don't have the vaguest idea how to go about doing it."

"Maybe you need a little more time to clear your head," he suggested. "After all, it's only been a few days since your breakup."

She paused, considering his suggestion. "You might be right. I definitely have a lot of cobwebs obstructing my vision. Nothing has looked right to me from behind the lens in a long time." *Not since the Five. Not since Mary.* "I can't seem to connect with my subjects. Definitely not these politicians with their phony smiles and empty promises."

He smiled. "There you go again with your strong aversion to politics."

Scottie winced. She needed to stop being so strong-minded about her opinions. "You'll be relieved to know I've ordered a vice grip for my mouth. I'm expecting it to arrive any day." Unable to help herself, she added, "But you have to admit I'm right. Reporters have scrutinized every aspect of the candidates' lives. They've investigated them from every angle. As parents and politicians. Their personal convictions and work ethics. Thanks to the constant media coverage, the American people already know everything there is to know about our nominees. And they've photographed them every which way but naked."

Guy burst into laughter. "I think you've identified your opportunity for a big break. I can see it now—photographs of Catherine Caine in the nude going viral on every social media outlet in the country."

Her eyes twinkled with excitement. "And you, Mr. Secret Service Agent, are just the man who can sneak me into her hotel room."

His face grew serious. "I never said I worked for the Secret Service. That is something you"—he pointed at her—"conjured up in your own mind. If you want to know the truth—"

Raised voices from the bar prevented Guy from finishing his sentence. An attractive woman, whom Scottie guessed to be in her late thirties, was arguing with her equally attractive, much-older date, her husband judging from the rock on her left hand.

Oblivious to attentive ears around him, the husband said, "You're only voting for a Democrat because she's a woman! Mark my word, the first time she has a hot flash, Catherine Caine will press the big red button and start a nuclear war."

His wife slammed her martini glass down on the bar. "You're an ignorant pig! You don't deserve to have the right to vote." She grabbed her bag and marched out of the restaurant, leaving her husband alone at the bar.

Guy let out a soft whistle. "There you have it—the proof of why a man should never marry outside his party."

Scottie's mouth flew open. "What a chauvinist thing to say! Not to mention a huge exaggeration. You don't seriously think that, do you?"

"Hell yes, I do. We don't discuss politics in my house, not since my parents nearly divorced over the issue of hanging chads in the Bush versus Gore election in 2000."

Scottie stared at him. "You're making that up."

He held up his hand, making the three-fingered salute of the Boy Scouts. "I swear to you I'm not."

"I'm sorry, but that's taking things too far. I don't mean any disrespect to your parents, I don't even know them, but for intelligent people to be incapable of carrying on a friendly debate is uncivilized. That's what's wrong with this country. We spend too much time arguing over things that don't matter and worrying about being politically correct, and not enough time discussing the real issues."

"You make a valid point."

"I'm tired of thinking about politics. Let's talk about

something else for a change." She propped her elbows on the table and rested her chin in her hands. "Tell me about growing up on the ranch?"

Sipping their way through the pitcher of beer, she peppered him with questions about his family and life on the ranch. She sensed he was holding back on her, that something in his family's past saddened him a great deal. But she cautioned herself not to pry. At least until she knew him better. And she hoped like hell she got the chance to know him better. She enjoyed his company. She felt connected to him in a way she hadn't to another human being in a long time. She found the conversation between them playful and teasing one minute and serious the next. In the dim light, his gray eyes reminded her of fog creeping over the Blue Ridge Mountains at daybreak. His sexy smile gave her tingly feelings in her tummy, and the brush of his knee against hers sent shock waves to parts of her body that had been numb for far too long. She was gearing up to ask Guy back to Amy's condo for a sleepless night of uninhibited sex when his cell phone rang.

He listened intently for several long minutes to the person on the other end. "I'll be there as soon as I can," he said and hung up. He signaled the waitress for the bill. "I gotta go."

"What happened?" Scottie asked, searching in her bag for her wallet.

"A member of the audience, some drunken Texan, got out of control during the keynote and started yelling derogatory insults at Byron Caine about his wife."

"What? That's crazy." Scottie's mind raced with thoughts of missed opportunities. "I didn't see anything happen, or even hear them say anything about it on TV."

"That's because they were able to keep the cameras off the man while they hauled him off."

Scottie placed her credit card along with his on top of the check. "Are you going back out to the Liberty Center tonight?"

"Unfortunately, I don't have much choice. Duty calls."

He tried to give her back her credit card but she insisted they split the bill.

"There's probably nothing left for me to report on, but will you text me if anything comes up?" she asked.

"Sure. Tell me your number and I'll send you a text so you'll have mine."

She called out the number, and he thumbed it into his phone. She received a funny face emoji from him seconds later.

"I'm sorry, Scottie. This is all on me. If only I hadn't made you leave the Liberty Center."

"I'm a big girl, Guy. I made that decision on my own."

They said goodnight on the sidewalk outside the restaurant. Despite Guy's preoccupation with the drunken man from Texas, Scottie had hoped for a kiss, even a quick brush on the lips. Instead, she received a peck on the forehead and a farewell that sounded like goodbye forever.

"Don't give up, Scottie. You'll get your big break. Remember, everybody has a story and everyone is keeping a secret. Some are just better at hiding them than others."

His Uber arrived and he left her standing on the sidewalk wondering what secret he was hiding.

10

SCOTTIE SLEPT FITFULLY that night, tossing and turning and wondering where she'd gone wrong with Guy, if she'd misread the lust in his smoldering gray eyes. The Drunken Texan episode didn't seem like that big of a deal. Was he really needed at the Liberty Center or was he just using the situation as an excuse to get away from her?

What did she really know about Guy Jordan, aside from what little he'd told her about his family?

She fixed herself a cup of coffee and crawled back in Amy's bed with her laptop. She googled Guy Jordan and a long list of bios and faces appeared, none of them belonging to the Guy she knew. Her search on Facebook rendered results, if you call an outdated profile picture and neglected page a success. According to his bio, he still attended the University of North Carolina at Chapel Hill, and was in a relationship with a girl named Sarah Shaw, who Scottie assumed was the raven-haired beauty in most of his pictures.

Perplexed about Guy's past and realizing she needed to get moving, she decided to take a power run through downtown Philly and then get a shower. Ninety minutes later, dressed and ready for the day, Scottie made an out-of-the-way trip to Knead

Bagels on her way to the Liberty Center. As soon as she entered the lobby, she scanned the sea of dark suits milling about, looking for Guy. Many of the men wore crew cuts, but few of them had his muscular build.

Guy's words played over in her mind—*I never said I worked for the Secret Service. That is something you conjured up in your own mind. If you want to know the truth—"*

The couple arguing over politics had interrupted Guy as he was about to leak vital information about himself. If not Secret Service, then what? Homeland Security? Perhaps he worked for the Democratic Party. Although that didn't explain why he'd attended the Republican convention. Surely he would have fessed up to being a politician during one of their many political discussions.

Scottie tried to shake off her concerns. No point in worrying about it when she was never going to see him again.

She forced herself to focus on her work. With mostly humorous commentary, photographs of the Drunken Texan had been popping up on all the social media sites throughout the morning. And to think she could've been in on the action if she hadn't been preoccupied with trying to woo a certain sexy cowboy into her bed.

She moved from one location to the next in the convention center, parking herself in whatever empty seat she could find that would offer her the best vantage points for watching the attendees. She studied the party leaders in their sleek attire with their fake smiles, wondering what skeletons resided in their closets—who was sleeping with whom and which ones engaged in unethical politics.

Everybody has a story, and everyone is keeping a secret, Guy had said.

She found the random attendees intriguing, those who didn't

hold political office—the delegates elected to nominate the candidate on behalf of the constituents in their state and the special interest groups invited to the convention to garner support for the Democratic Party. She pondered the crippling disease that had left the twelve-year-old girl from Kentucky in a wheelchair, and imagined the land mind that had torn off both of the young Marine's legs.

As she whiled away the long afternoon, Scottie thought a lot about life and how the choices we make determine the people we become. Not everyone is born with the same moral compass. She contemplated her own story and the decisions she'd made that had not served her well, namely her marriage to Brad. And she thought about the secrets she'd kept. She thought about Mary. Experience had taught her that honest people did bad things for good reasons.

Covering politics was not the best choice for her if exposing scandals paved the path to success. And she could no longer stomach the mass shootings—Americans killing Americans on American soil. She longed to report on honest, hard-working people, struggling to cope in their everyday lives. She wanted a job with a boss who offered her assignments in remote parts of the world, but she feared she would never be anything more than a wedding photographer. In which case she'd be the best damn wedding photographer in Richmond. She'd rent a studio on Grove Avenue and take head shots of professionals for their websites and group photographs of families for their annual Christmas card.

Scottie stayed until the bitter end of the convention, terrified she might miss an opportunity to report on another Drunken Texan. Catherine Caine's acceptance speech had a profound impact on her. Scottie was impressed by Caine's record in the Senate, moved by her concern for the American people, and inspired by her enthusiasm. By the time Caine had finished her speech, Scottie was considering casting her own vote for the Democratic Party nominee. This unique woman struck Scottie as having the qualities to bring about necessary changes for the country. If anyone could restore her faith in politics, Catherine Caine might just be the one.

If only Scottie could find a way to get up close and personal to the senator. *And they've photographed them every which way but naked.* Sneaking into Caine's hotel room was out of the question, not that Scottie would ever consider taking images of her in the nude, but there was nothing wrong with sticking close to her in the hopes of capturing a candid moment.

While Caine gathered with her family on stage to greet the nation, Scottie fought her way through the crowd to the front of the auditorium, and then headed for the exit doors that presumably led to the back of the convention center. Two female Secret Service agents stood with their backs to Scottie. They appeared to be caught up in the moment, their post forgotten as they watched the candidate celebrate with her family. Scottie slipped undetected through the double doors, jogged down a short hallway, and exited the building through the rear entrance.

She was surprised to find the back alleyway deserted, although she could see Secret Servicemen stationed on the streets that ran perpendicular at both ends. The building on the other side of the alley was a theater of some sort—closed for business during the convention, its double doors chained and padlock against intruders. Two spotlights above the doors on both buildings provided dim illumination for the alley.

Hugging the wall, Scottie inched to the right ten feet to where a small green dumpster overflowed with trash. She stuffed her blonde hair under a navy UVA cap, adjusted the settings on her camera, and squatted down behind the dumpster. Her dark jeans and black tunic gave her a head start on blending in to the surroundings. But additional protection couldn't hurt. She covered herself as best she could with loose bags of trash, leaving enough room to see and breathing through her mouth in an effort to minimize the stench of rotting garbage.

While her behavior bordered on stalking, she saw no harm in snapping a quick photograph of the candidate with her family from afar. Considering her press credentials, worst case scenario, all the Secret Servicemen would do is ask her to leave.

The lack of security puzzled her. Surely the Secret Service planned to sweep the alley ahead of the senator's departure from the Liberty Center. Unless Caine planned to exit the building through the front entrance. But that seemed unlikely considering the mobs of people swarming the lobby on their way out.

Fifteen minutes passed. And then another ten. She was ready to abandon her plan and go home when two Secret Servicemen appeared from inside. Both men, their heads shaved, wore dark suits. The bald look worked well for the taller agent. Not so much for the shorter, less attractive man.

Shorty passed within five feet of Scottie on his first walk-through of the alley, but stopped to take a closer look on his way back. The beam from his flashlight passed within inches of her head.

"What's up with all this trash?" Shorty called out to his partner.

"Some mix-up with the city. They were supposed to empty the dumpster twice during the convention instead of their usual once-a-week routine. No need to worry. We had a crew check it out earlier."

"If you say so." Shorty gave the bags of trash a quick kick, somewhere close to Scottie's ribs, before continuing on with his search.

When the agents finally gave the all clear, the candidate's

family streamed out of the building in single file. Four generations of the Caine family crowded the alley, laughing and cheering, celebrating the senator's nomination for president of the United States.

Two stretch limos arrived on the scene, parking one in front of the other. Chauffeurs wearing black suits and white gloves stepped from the driver's side and opened the rear doors for their passengers.

When no one made a move to get in, the candidate's son, John Jacob Caine IV, known to the country as Jake, asked the group, "Where's Mom? Isn't she coming with us?"

Scottie heard a female voice say, "She's wrapping up some loose ends. She'll meet us at the reception later."

"Okay, then. What are we waiting for?" Jake clapped his hands to get his family's attention. "Everybody pile in. Old people in the first car and the youngsters in the second."

The Caine family climbed into the limos amid a flurry of activity—feet kicking, purses flying, doors slamming. The chauffeurs returned to their respective limos and sped off, exiting at the other end of the alley.

When the Secret Service agents made no move to reenter the building, Scottie assumed they were waiting for Senator Caine to appear. One of them lit a cigarette, and she knew she was in for a long wait. She tried to ignore the cramp in her left calf muscle, the smell of stale coffee and sour milk at her nose. She managed to bring the camera close enough to her face to double-check the screen, making certain the shutter speed and aperture would accommodate the dark setting. She waited for what seemed like an hour, but was probably only fifteen minutes, before another black limo whipped around the corner from Broad Street and screeched to a halt twenty feet from her hiding place. The taller of the Secret Servicemen tapped on the driver's window. The window rolled down and the driver exchanged words with the agent out of Scottie's earshot. The agent nodded his head and stepped back into place beside his partner.

Ten more minutes passed. Then everything happened at once. The chauffeur, a giant of a man, got out of the car and opened the rear door for his passenger. A gentleman in his late fifties, dressed in light-colored slacks and a slate-blue linen sport coat, emerged from the backseat. Scottie, observing his deep tan and head full of salt-and-pepper hair, thought he might be the most elegant man she'd ever seen. The back door of the convention center then flew open and the senator walked out, followed by an attractive woman in her late twenties. The Secret Servicemen stepped aside, watching as Caine walked straight into the gentleman's outstretched arms.

Without taking time to consider the ramifications of her actions, Scottie rose from her hiding place, focused her zoom lens, and held the shutter button down while her camera captured the embrace, the kiss, and the subjects' shocked expressions in one continuous stream of photographs.

When he finally noticed Scottie, Shorty yelled, "Hey! What do you think you're doing?"

Scottie took off running toward the street.

"Get that girl! Don't let her out of your sight!"

With their backs facing the alley, the agents positioned on the street didn't hear Shorty's cry for help in time to respond. Barreling past them, Scottie rounded the corner of the convention center and sprinted down the sidewalk. The agents were fast on her trail, their feet pounding the pavement behind her, but they were no match for her pace. She was in top shape—still held her high school's record for the 55m dash and went on power runs as often as she could.

Scottie, snatching the baseball cap off her head and tossing her long blonde hair over her shoulder, soon lost herself in the mob of people gathered on the sidewalk at the front of the building. She crossed the street on the north side of the convention center, weaving in and out of the waiting taxis, and then ducked inside a crowded bar. After fighting her way through to the kitchen and out the back door, she saw a few pedestrians, stragglers from the convention she assumed, idling about on the street. But no men in dark suits raced toward her. Casting frequent glances over her shoulder, she jogged west one block to the nearest subway station.

*

When she reached the safety of the condo, Scottie double-bolted the door. She went straight to the refrigerator and grabbed the bottle of Pinot Grigio that she'd purchased for Amy as a thank you gift for letting her stay there. She poured herself a glass of wine and then collapsed onto the sofa, sinking into the down cushions.

Holy shit! What just happened?

For the next few minutes, Scottie replayed the scene over and over in her mind—the greeting, the surprise, the chase. Her nerves on end, she jumped to her feet again and went to the window, staring down at the empty street below. No one appeared to have followed her. She yanked the blinds closed.

Think, Scottie, think. She slumped back against the wall.

Aside from being an obnoxious photographer in hot pursuit of her prey, she hadn't done anything wrong, at least not as far as she knew. She'd gotten her shot all right, her big break, the one photograph that would make her career. But at what cost to her integrity? She'd been chased out of a dark alley like a common criminal. She failed herself. She'd vowed a long time ago never to resort to the reprehensible tactics of the paparazzi.

And what about the senator? How dare Catherine Caine sneak off with another man while her family, her husband and children and grandchildren, were celebrating her most crowning achievement at some hospitality room in a nearby hotel. How could Caine cheat on her husband? This woman who represented the people of the Commonwealth of Massachusetts. This woman who held her audiences spellbound with her ideas of how to make our country better for the next generation. This woman who was running for president of the United States—whom, only moments earlier, Scottie had considered voting for. This woman was no better than Brad. When would the lying, cheating, and backstabbing ever end?

Scottie imagined Caine's team gathered around a conference table, drinking coffee and scrutinizing surveillance video from the alley. The photographs she took tonight could damage the candidate's reputation and ruin the election for the Democrats. With one email, she could entice a dozen buyers willing to pay big bucks for the images. With one phone call, she could destroy the careers of many. How much time did she have before Caine's people came looking for her? Was it even safe for her to go home? They would have to identify her first. She'd been wearing dark clothing and a ball cap pulled down over her face. Whether they got a clear shot of her depended on the angle of the surveillance camera.

She removed the memory card from her camera and inserted it into her laptop. The images loaded on the screen. Twelve of the fifteen shots were blurry, but three captured the exchange in sharp detail. She pored over the images, trying to make sense of it all. The embrace. The kiss. The shocked expressions, wide eyes and o-shaped mouths, when her subjects realized someone had encroached upon their private moment. Who was the man anyway, this elegant stranger in the photograph with the candidate?

The images screamed romance, but Scottie's gut warned her to tread carefully, that appearances might be deceiving in this case.

She spent the next several hours scouring the Internet for photographs of the senator's family and friends and business associates she'd been involved with throughout the years. She studied photographs taken during Caine's time at Exeter and Harvard, and hundreds of images of members of Congress, both in the Senate and the House of Representatives. When she failed to find the mystery man in any of the photographs, she used every image search tool she could find, hoping to match the dazzling smile and piercing blue eyes of the handsome stranger.

She finally gave up around four. Wired from too much coffee, realizing there would be no sleep for her that night, Scottie decided to take advantage of the remaining hours of darkness and head back to Richmond. She stripped off her clothes and was stepping into Amy's shower when she caught sight of her press pass tangled up with her black tunic on the floor. She picked up the pass and ran her finger across her name printed on the card.

How could you be so stupid?

11

THE FOUR-HOUR DRIVE home gave Scottie a chance to ponder her dilemma, and as much as she wanted to taste the glory of success, to be the photographer to bring the presidential election to a screeching halt, her conscience prevented her from contacting her news sources until she identified the stranger, until she knew for certain the man wasn't Catherine Caine's third cousin twice removed.

With seventy-nine percent relative humidity and temperatures soaring near a hundred, Scottie broke out into a sweat the minute she stepped from her car in front of her house. Slinging her bags over her shoulder, she trudged up the sidewalk to her front door, surprised to find it slightly ajar. Her immediate thought was that Will or her parents had stopped by, but she'd forgotten to give either of them a spare key that fit the new locks. After their talk at the farm, she didn't think Brad would break in, but his drug usage had made his behavior unpredictable lately. Pushing the door open, she called, "Brad, are you in here?"

An eerie silence greeted her.

Taking a deep breath, she stepped across the threshold and into the foyer. The devastation in her living room sent shivers down her spine. Whoever had broken in had overturned most of the furniture and ripped apart the pillows from her sofa. Feathers covered nearly every surface. Her nineteenth-century Rose Medallion vase that once stood proudly on the mantle lay shattered in pieces on the hearth. A surge of anger pumped through her body, but was quickly replaced by fear. Throwing beer bottles at the exterior of her house was one thing, but she didn't think her husband would destroy her most prized possession. The process of elimination led to only one possible scenario. Whoever had broken into her house was looking for the digital image files of Caine and her mystery man.

She dumped her duffel onto the floor beside the stairs, but held tight to her electronics bag, the bag that held the evidence the intruder wanted. Leaving the front door wide open, she tiptoed down the hall where more destruction awaited her in the kitchen and family rooms. Grabbing the sharpest knife from the block on the counter, she searched both floors room by room, checking every closet and under every bed. Satisfied the house was empty, she locked the front door and texted her brother: *Someone broke into my house. Can you come over?*

He texted back: *On my way.*

When she greeted him at the door fifteen minutes later, after a quick glance up and down the street, Scottie yanked Will inside and locked the door behind her.

"What the hell, Scottie? You're acting paranoid." Then he caught sight of the mess in the living room. "Brad, that asshole. Did you call the police?"

"Brad didn't do this. He came out to the farm on Sunday to see me. We made nice."

Will raised his eyebrows in question. "You made *nice?*"

"You know what I mean. As nice as two people can be who are getting divorced."

"I don't understand." He motioned toward the living room. "Who would want to ransack your house if not Brad?"

"People looking for some photographs I took."

"I don't like the sound of that," he said. "What kind of mess have you gotten yourself into this time, Scott?"

"A big one. So what else is new?"

Will rubbed the back of his neck. "I guess you'd better show me the photographs."

"They're on my computer in the kitchen."

He followed her to the back of the house.

She closed the plantation shutters, not that a stranger could get passed the yipping Yorkie Terrors in the backyard next door. She set her laptop on the kitchen counter and accessed Lightroom. The image of Catherine Caine kissing the stranger filled the screen.

Will glanced at the photograph, and then did a double take. "Whoa! That's Senator Caine." He leaned in closer to the computer. "That's not her husband though, is it?"

"I've been on the Internet all night trying to identify this man. I've studied every photograph ever taken of Catherine Caine, and I can assure you that is not her husband. I have no idea who he is." Scottie scrolled through the three pictures, pausing to give her brother a chance to examine each one.

Will rubbed his eyes with his balled fist as if to clear them. "Where and when did you take these?"

"I took them last night in the alley behind the convention center after Caine's acceptance speech."

Will's mouth fell open. "You mean to tell me you just waltzed into a dark alley, marched up to the presidential candidate, and said cheese?"

She shook her head. "I didn't waltz, march, or say cheese. I hid behind a row of trashcans."

"Where the hell was the Secret Service?"

"They were there, in the alley, but they didn't see me. I was wearing dark clothing and a baseball cap pulled down over my head, covering my face."

"Didn't they sweep the alley?"

"I guess. If you want to call their lame walk-through a sweep." Scottie went to the refrigerator and poured two glasses of sweet tea. "Here, sit,"—she handed him a glass—"and I'll tell you the whole story."

For the next ten minutes, she fed him blow-by-blow details of the events in the alley and subsequent chase.

When she finished talking, Will said, "Since I haven't seen anything about any of this on the news today, I'm guessing you haven't sold the photographs."

"Not yet. I haven't decided what to do." She slid the computer in front of him. "Look at them closely. Tell me what you see."

He scrolled back and forth, inspecting each photograph closely. "The man's kiss is close enough to Caine's lips to suggest familiarity, but it's not a full-fledged kiss like lovers have." He clicked to the next shot. "Same thing with the embrace. A friendly greeting, but not necessarily one that exudes passion." He closed the laptop. "As far as whether or not Senator Caine is romantically involved with this man, I'd have to say the evidence is inconclusive. I would love for it to be true, because a scandal like this would ruin the election for the Democrats. But based on the images, I don't think you should assume these two people are having an affair."

"That's what I thought too, until an hour ago when I came home and found my house torn apart." She waved her hand at the computer. "Why would someone break into my house looking for the digital files unless they had something to hide?"

"And you assume that someone is Senator Caine?"

"Or one of her team members," Scottie said. "The Democratic Party has the most to lose if those photos go viral."

Will pursed his lips in thought. "I'm not sure you can say that with absolute certainty until you know who this man is. He may have as much at stake as Caine does."

"I seriously doubt that. He's not a congressman. I went through all five hundred and thirty-five of them. He's not a Fortune 500 corporate exec or on the Forbes list of the richest people in the world."

"Hmm." Will scratched his chin as he considered the possibilities. "Maybe he's a big donor who prefers to remain anonymous?"

"He's definitely anonymous," Scottie said. "The man doesn't exist. At least not as far as the Internet is concerned."

Will brought his fingers to his forehead. "Off the top of my head, I can think of ten different scenarios why a wealthy man would want to protect his identity. He could be English royalty, fifth in line for the throne. Or a Saudi Arabian oil baron. Or a South African diamond miner."

"Yes!" She smacked the counter with the palms of her hands. "The more prestigious the man, the juicier my story will be. I can see the headlines now: *Senator Catherine Caine Has Romantic Interlude with Wealthy Playboy.*"

"Don't get ahead of yourself, Scott. You need to carefully consider how you proceed. Whoever it is you are dealing with already broke the law by breaking into your house. Do you realize your life might be in danger?"

"No one wants to hurt me," she said. "They just want to get their hands on the digital files."

"Then why not sell the photographs to ABC News and be done with it?" Will suggested. "Going public with the images will remove the pot of gold from the lion's den."

"And miss out on my big chance? No way. If Catherine

Caine is in fact having an affair with this man, someone will eventually break the story. And I want that someone to be me."

Will buried his face in his hands in frustration. After a minute, when a thought struck him, he looked back up at her. "You said earlier that you were wearing dark clothing and a baseball hat. How did these people who broke into your house identify you so quickly?"

Scottie removed her press pass from her camera bag and dropped it on the counter. "Exhibit A."

Will picked up the press pass. "Please tell me you weren't wearing this in the alley."

She shrugged. "I forgot I had it on. My goal was to get a family friendly photo of the senator, not rock the biggest scandal in American politics since Monica Lewinsky had oral sex with Bill Clinton in the Oval Office."

"There you go getting ahead of yourself again. You need to do your homework before you break the story. I'm sure this encounter is easily explained."

"Give me a little credit, Will. I'm a professional. I have every intention of investigating the situation. But I have a gut feeling about this. And my ransacked house is evidence that there is more to this encounter than meets the eye." Scottie slid the computer in front of her and began saving files.

"Listen to me, Scottie. You can't handle this situation alone." Will's voice was full of desperation. "You need to call the FBI or the local authorities. Why don't you simply go to Caine directly and ask for an exclusive interview in exchange for the files?"

She slammed the laptop shut and hopped off her bar stool. Grabbing a handful of Will's shirt, she dragged him to his feet. "Thanks for coming over, little bro, but you need to go now." She took his hand and led him down the hall to the foyer.

"What are you planning, Scottie?"

"I'm a sitting duck here, waiting for Caine's people to come after me. I'm going to DC. I know someone there who can help me identify this man. By the way"—she removed a key from the drawer in the small table beside the front door—"I had my locks changed last week when I kicked Brad out. Here's the new spare."

"Just in case I have time this weekend to clean this mess up?"

"Don't you dare," she said, smacking him on the chest with the back of her hand. "This mess isn't going anywhere. I'll deal with it when I get home."

Will removed her old spare from his key ring and replaced it with the new one. "Aren't you leaving for the Olympics soon?"

She shook her head. "Not until next week. We'll have pizza night before I go."

Will reached for the doorknob, but then stopped and turned to her, his face serious. "Promise me you'll call me, no matter what time or where you are, if you get in over your head."

"You have no reason to worry about me."

"Ha. Since when?"

"Okay, you have plenty of reason to worry about me, based on my poor decisions of late, but I promise I'll be careful. And I'll call you at the first sign of trouble."

"I don't believe you, but okay. Do you need any money?"

"Now you sound like Dad." She opened the door and shoved him out onto the stoop. "But I appreciate your concern more than you know."

She closed the door behind him and wheeled her small suitcase up the stairs. The vandalism to the upstairs rooms was even more disheartening for Scottie. *What kind of person destroys a baby's nursery?* She closed the door and vowed to dismantle the room and give the furniture to charity as soon as she returned home from the Olympics. Sorting through the clothes strewn across her bedroom, she removed the dirty ones from her suitcase and stuffed it full with clean T-shirts and jeans.

She returned to her laptop in the kitchen and made two password-protected copies of the image files, saving one on each of her cloud drives. She exported another copy of the files to a thumb drive, which she hid in the box of tampons in her suitcase where no man would dare to search. With a pair of scissors, she cut a small slit in the lining of her electronics bag and slipped the memory card with the original raw image files inside. She would have to tear the bag apart in order to get the memory card out.

If it came to that, she was in more trouble than her brother could bail her out of.

12

SCOTTIE WAS STOWING her bags in her car when Will called. "I'm pretty sure someone followed me back to work. You are in over your head, Scott. Call the police. Now."

She slammed the rear door and slid into the driver's seat. "I'm sorry, but I can't do that. What kind of investigative reporter would I be if I called the police?"

"A safe one. You are playing a very dangerous game, and you need to get some help."

"Which is why I'm heading to DC. You've got to stop worrying about me so much."

"That's hard to do considering your track record."

"I'll be fine. Gotta go now. I'll text you from DC." She ended the call.

As soon as she pulled away from the curb, a nondescript sedan fell in behind her. The one distinguishing feature on the four-door, gray Ford Taurus was the blue and gold Pennsylvania license plates.

Scottie made a right-hand turn at the Stop sign. When the Ford followed her, she took a quick left and another hard right. Sure enough, the Ford stuck close to her bumper. At the next red light, through the rearview mirror, she caught a glimpse of the large man who was driving. His face was hidden behind dark glasses and a baseball cap. She saw the shadow of a figure in the passenger seat, but she couldn't make out the features enough to tell whether the person was male or female.

I know this town a lot better than you do, buddy. When the light turned green, she sped off down Eighth Street. Zipping around downtown, weaving in and out of traffic, she gained distance on the Taurus, although she could still see him in her rearview mirror struggling to keep up. She zoomed down Canal Street and worked her way over to Hollywood Cemetery. The Taurus was closing in on her when she passed through the main gates. She raced past the row of mausoleums beside the river and careened up the hill just beyond Jefferson Davis's gravesite. Scottie knew Hollywood better than her own neighborhood from the frequent visits to her grandparents' graves. She quickly lost her pursuers in the hundred-plus acres of valleys and hills that served as the final resting place for two American presidents and thousands of Confederate soldiers—including twenty-two generals. Departing the cemetery from the other side, she got on the downtown expressway, and with frequent glances in her rearview mirror, headed up Interstate 95 toward Washington.

Scottie was ten miles outside of town when she realized Guy's cell number was the only contact information she had for him. She had no idea who he worked for or where he lived. She exited the interstate in Ashland and drove to the nearest shopping center where she located an ATM machine and withdrew the balance in her checking account. Other than the money she needed for her trip to Rio, which was tucked away in her savings account, she was flat broke. Crossing the highway to a convenience store, she filled her tank with gas and purchased a turkey sandwich and a Diet Coke from inside the store. She sat in her car in the parking lot composing her text to Guy while she ate her lunch. She kept the tone professional so as not to give him the wrong idea.

Sorry I missed you at the convention yesterday. I'm on my way to DC and would like to meet with you privately about an urgent matter. I look forward to hearing from you regarding your availability.

She set her cell phone in the center console, with the screen facing up, to await his response.

Without Guy, she didn't have a plan. Even if he didn't work for the Secret Service or the Department of Homeland Security, he might know someone with access to software that might identify Caine's mystery man.

She was nearing Alexandria and beginning to worry she wouldn't hear from him when she received his text: *I'm wrapping things up at work. I'll meet you at my apartment in an hour.* He included the address of his apartment building on Massachusetts Avenue near Logan Circle.

She drove willy-nilly around the DC business district until she was certain no one was following her. She parked her Mini in Guy's parking deck and went inside the lobby to wait for him. He arrived ninety minutes later.

"I'm sorry. I got caught up in a meeting." He led her by the elbow to the elevator. "Let's go up to my apartment where we can talk."

They rode up to the fourth floor, and then walked down the hallway to his apartment. He unlocked the door and stepped aside for her to enter. "It's small but works for me. I prefer to live alone, so I can't afford much."

The main living space included a kitchen and sitting room, which also served as his home office judging from the messy desk in the corner. What Scottie assumed was the master bedroom opened off to the side. She felt like she was on her family's farm amongst the leather furniture and oriental rugs. Her eyes traveled to the set of bull horns on the wall over his bedroom door. "A souvenir from the ranch, I presume?"

He laughed. "Something like that. Have a seat." He motioned to the sofa and they sat down side by side. "Tell me how I can help."

"I'm working on a story, and I could use your help in verifying some of the details."

Settling back on the sofa, he threaded his fingers together and placed his hands in his lap. "Go on, I'm listening."

"Before I explain, I need to know I can trust you, that this conversation doesn't leave this room."

He smiled. "Whatever is said on the ranch stays on the ranch."

"I'm serious, Guy. Important people could get hurt if I don't handle this situation properly."

"Now I'm really intrigued." He locked eyes with her. "We don't know each other very well, Scottie, but I promise you, you can trust me. Whatever you tell me does not leave this apartment without your permission."

A wave of doubt gripped her. Someone had ransacked her home and chased her through the streets of downtown Richmond. Was she making the wrong decision by sharing her story with a man she barely knew? Maybe. But if Guy wouldn't help her, she didn't know anyone else who could.

She removed her laptop from her bag and placed it in her lap. "Last night at the convention, I stumbled into a bit of a predicament."

"Define *stumble*."

"Okay… So maybe it's more accurate to say I was lying in wait in the alley behind the convention center."

His eyes grew big and round.

"I know." She sighed. "Call me the paparazzi, but I was

desperate for a shot of Catherine Caine alone with her family, just one photograph that was different from all the rest."

"And I assume you got it?"

"Oh, yeah. Three of them." She set her laptop on the coffee table in front of them, loaded the images, and watched closely for his initial reaction. His gray eyes lit up for a brief second, like the sun beaming through a cloudy sky, but just as quickly, his expression turned serious.

"Who's the guy?"

She considered a witty *that guy* comeback, and then realized it wasn't appropriate. "I haven't a clue. I was awake half the night searching the Internet. He doesn't exist, at least not on social media, or anywhere else online for that matter."

He leaned in for a closer view. "He's dressed like he's going to dinner at a five-star resort. His clothes aren't flashy, but well cut. Clearly he has money."

"He's wealthy, all right. There's no doubt in my mind. His grooming is immaculate. Look at his hands." Scottie zoomed in on the man's manicured hands. "He's elegant. Some might even call him debonair."

Guy shot her a sideways glance. "You make him sound like James Bond."

Scottie considered herself something of an expert on Bond. Her soon-to-be ex-husband owned every movie in the collection. "Bond is actually a good analogy. Add a few gray hairs at the temples, and he would pass for Pierce Brosnan any day."

"Brosnan, huh? Why not Roger Moore or Sean Connery?"

She rolled her eyes. "Will you be serious?"

Guy returned his attention to the computer. "Why haven't you sold the photographs?"

"My conscience won't let me until I know who he is. I don't want to end up with mud dripping from my face by posting my photographs without the facts. If he turns out to be Catherine Caine's best friend from kindergarten days, I'll look like an idiot."

"You have a photograph of a strange man kissing the Democratic candidate for president. Who cares who he is, as long as he's not her brother?" Guy examined the photographs closely. "I've met both her brothers several times. And I can assure you, that man is neither Samuel nor Lawrence Wainwright. You're a photojournalist, Scottie. You're only responsible for the image. Why don't you submit your pictures and let the news folks figure out who he is?"

"I'm more than a photojournalist, Guy. If I want top news organizations to consider me for positions that will take me to the places I want to go, I need to submit the complete package. Both the story and the image must have my byline."

"And you think I'm in a position to help you determine this man's identity?"

She nodded. "I thought that maybe you, or someone you know, might have access to certain databases…"

"We don't live in a totalitarian state, Scottie. Our government doesn't have constant surveillance on the American people any more than we have a database that catalogs every citizen's image. If this man is a criminal, then that's a different story. Did you ever think these pictures might place you in danger?"

She looked away from him, not wanting to see his reaction when she told him her house had been broken into and she'd been chased. "Actually, I already have a couple of thugs harassing me."

His face fell. "You conveniently left that part out."

She told him about the men who had ransacked her house and chased her through downtown Richmond.

He moved to the edge of the sofa, closer to her. "Listen to me, Scottie. This is a dangerous situation, and I'm not sure I'm the right person to help you. My involvement in your crisis presents a conflict of interest on a number of different levels."

Scottie jumped to her feet. "I may never get a chance like this again, Guy. If you can't help me, I don't know anyone else who can."

He stared at her for several long seconds, then let out a deep breath and said, "I need a minute to think about it."

When he stood up and walked over to the window, Scottie leaned against the kitchen counter and watched the minutes tick away on the oven clock. Five minutes, then ten. She held her breath when he finally turned to face her, his expression all business.

"I have a few colleagues I can ask for advice. If you're okay with it, I'll show them the pictures and see what they think. They may even know who the man is."

She tilted her head to the side as she considered his response. "You don't work for the Secret Service or the Department of Homeland Security, do you?"

"No. I most definitely do not."

"Then who? The GOP?"

"I—" He started to speak, then clammed up. "You're gonna have to trust me for now, if you want my help in identifying this Brosnan character."

Scottie gnawed on her lower lip. He didn't deny working for the Republican Party, which was the same as admitting to it in her book. He'd had plenty of opportunities to mention this little tidbit when they'd talked about politics during their previous two encounters. Would his allegiance to the GOP, to Andrew Blackmore if he was working on the presidential campaign, prevent him from handling the situation objectively? Did these *colleagues* of his also work for the Republican Party? She imagined a roomful of campaign workers gathered around a computer drooling over the images, discussing the ruination of their opponent. They would leak the photographs first and ask questions later. They didn't know Scottie. They wouldn't care about her integrity as a reporter.

She couldn't explain it, but something about Guy told Scottie she could trust him. And she'd made a vow to herself to pay more attention to her wise inner voice that usually proved to be spot on and ignore the reckless impulses that led her to trouble.

She sighed. "I guess it doesn't really matter who your boss is. You've already seen the photographs. The cat is out of the bag." She thought about it for a minute. "Okay, fine. I'll let you show the images to your colleagues, as long as they don't share them with anyone else." She downloaded the files onto yet another memory stick and handed it to him. "Leave the images on this drive. Whatever you do, do *not* copy them to anyone's computer or mobile device. And I want that memory stick back when you're done."

"Understood." He took the drive from her and slipped it in his pocket. He opened the door. "Lock this door behind me, and whatever you do, don't leave this apartment until I get back."

"Don't worry. I have nowhere to go."

13

GUY BYPASSED THE elevator and headed for the stairs, taking them two at a time down four flights. He jogged through the lobby and hit the sidewalk running. He weaved his way in between and around the afternoon commuters for six blocks, until he felt some of the tension leave his body.

Scottie Darden had turned his life upside down, one somersault at a time, ever since he met her a week ago at the Richmond airport. He'd finally managed to go for a stretch of time that afternoon without thinking about her once. Then boom, she showed up on his doorstep, asking for his help, with a handful of photographs that could guarantee him a job come January. Once the images went viral, the election would be over for Catherine Caine. Andrew Blackmore would become the next president of the United States, and Guy would be appointed chief of something. No way was he walking away from the opportunity. He considered himself a good guy, but he sure as hell was no saint.

At the next intersection, while he waited for traffic to clear, he sent a group text to his coworkers: *We have a 911. Meet me at the office asap.*

Rich replied: *We're still at the office, bro. What's up?*

I'll fill you in when I get there. ETA five mins.

Somehow Guy needed to figure out a solution that worked for all of them. He knew his coworkers well enough to realize that, when they saw these images, Rich and James would open a bottle of Jameson Reserve and call in the strippers. But they were a long way from celebrating. The outcome of this once in a lifetime opportunity hinged on all of them playing their cards right. Rich and James knew every insider in Washington by name. With any luck, they could identify the mystery man. And even better if they could explain his relationship with Senator Caine. If not, they would have to figure out a plan B that Guy could sell to Scottie. He agreed with her that leaking the photographs to the press without the story would be both political and professional suicide.

Rich and James were waiting at Guy's desk when he arrived. "What's up, man? We were just leaving to get some dinner."

"Order a pizza," Guy said, pulling his desk chair up to his computer. "We're gonna be a while."

He inserted the memory stick into his computer and clicked on the files. The faces of Senator Caine and her mystery man filled his screen.

"Holy shit!" James's blue eyes grew as big and round as SpongeBob's. "Is that who I think it is?"

"It's certainly not Mother Teresa." Guy scrolled through the images. "What I want to know is, who is the man kissing Senator Caine?"

Guy felt James and Rich breathing down his neck as they peered over his shoulder. "Can you zoom in a little?" Rich asked.

Guy magnified the image, and the three of them studied the mystery man's face.

"I haven't a clue," Rich said. "He looks familiar, like I've met him somewhere before, but I can't place him."

"He could be any one of a thousand campaign contributors

we've met over the past eighteen months," James added. "Where the hell did you get these images?"

"From a photojournalist I met last week when my plane rerouted to Richmond. I ran into her again in Philadelphia. She came to me this afternoon for help identifying this man." Guy filled them in on how Scottie had captured the images and the subsequent break in at her house.

James punched the air. "Whoo-hoo! This is the end of the road for the Democrats." He jabbed his finger at the computer. "Post those suckers online this instant."

Guy swiveled in his chair to face his coworkers. "Didn't you hear what I just said? These are not our photographs to leak. We have to play it Scottie's way. If we post them and it turns out this man is a close relative of the senator's, we will be eating a plateful of crow from now until the next presidential election in four years."

"They're romantically involved all right," Rich said. "Why else would someone have broken into her house?"

Guy rubbed his chin. "You make a good point, but we have to be absolutely certain."

James shook his head in disgust. "You'll never survive in politics with those kind of ethics."

"I agree with James," Rich said. "You need to post the pictures now and ask for forgiveness later from your new girlfriend... or whatever she is to you."

"Look, guys, I'm just as anxious as you are to stage a social media blitz with these images. But my daddy doesn't have deep pockets like yours. My reputation is all I've got. I gave Scottie my word, and I'm sticking to it."

"What do you suggest we do, then?" Rich asked. "We can't let this opportunity go."

Guy turned back around to his computer. "We find someone who can identify this man."

"Like who?" James asked, his tone skeptical.

"Surely we can think of somebody." Rich crossed his legs and leaned back against Guy's desk as he contemplated their dilemma. "What about Roger Baird? If he can't help us, I'm sure he knows someone who can."

Roger Baird was the hotshot young agent who had recently rocketed to the top of the FBI's food chain.

"Dude." James smacked Rich on the back. "Do you seriously know Roger Baird?"

Rich shrugged. "Enough to ask him for a favor. He dated my sister for a while in college."

"Then by all means, text him," James said, pointing at the cell phone in Rich's hand. "Get him over here now."

When Rich started to thumb a text, Guy said, "Don't text him, dumb ass. This situation warrants a phone call."

"Right." Rich clicked on the number and held the phone to his ear. He listened for a minute, and then left a brief message for Roger to call him regarding an urgent matter. He slammed his phone down on Guy's desk. "According to Roger's voice mail, he's not available until Monday."

"That's what happens when you get five promotions in two years—time off for good behavior." James hurled the pen he'd been holding across the room. "What are we supposed to do now, sit on this all weekend?"

"Unless you have a better idea," Guy said.

"Actually I do." Rich picked his phone back up. "Text me the images, Guy. I have an idea of where I might find Baird."

"I can't do that," Guy said, shaking his head. "I promised Scottie I wouldn't share them."

Rich's nostrils flared. "Look, dude. We need to divide and conquer on this. Go home to this Scottie person. Take her out to dinner. Show her a good time in bed. I don't care what you do with her. Just keep her safe and don't let her out of your sight no matter what. In the meantime, James and I will find a way to identify this man. But you've got to trust us with the image files in order to do that."

Guy thought about it for a minute. "I can't give you the full image, but I can give you something that will work just as well." He opened his photo editor and cropped Senator Caine out of the image that offered the clearest view of the mystery man. He exported the new file and texted it to Rich. "There. You should get it in a second. But I'm warning you, if one word of this leaks to the press, I'll know where it came from. And you'll have to answer to me."

14

AFTER GUY LEFT to meet with his coworkers, Scottie settled in at the bar with her laptop. She turned on CNN for background entertainment while she edited her photographs from the convention and uploaded them to her website. With two popular candidates for president, America was hopeful for new leadership, which meant patriotism was trending on social media. Scottie was pleased to see her Republican convention photographs flying off the shelves of her online store. She transferred her meager earnings from her PayPal account to her checking account, once again giving her a positive balance.

Around eight o'clock, when her stomach started to growl, her turkey sandwich now a dim memory, she inspected the slim pickings in Guy's refrigerator—cartons of moldy leftover Chinese food, a package of individually wrapped process cheese slices, and a half-empty jar of dill pickles. She didn't dare leave the safety of Guy's building, not that the goon platoon could possibly have followed her. Instead, she tried to curb her appetite by drinking three tumblers full of water.

Curling up on the sofa, she surfed the news networks and caught up on the latest headlines, election related and otherwise. She was in a semiconscious state, seconds away from drifting off to sleep, when Guy got home a few minutes before ten. "Dinner." He held up a brown paper bag spotted with grease. "Burgers and fries from Hal's, the best hangover dive in the city."

"What if I don't have a hangover?" she asked.

"The plan is to eat the burgers in advance of the hangovers we're going to have tomorrow." He produced a bottle of Grey Goose from the cabinet under his television. He poured two shots and handed her one. "Cheers." He held his glass out to her. "To identifying the mystery man."

She downed her shot and dug into the burger bag. "I'm starving." She removed two foil-wrapped burgers and a handful of plastic condiment packages. "Are both of them the same?"

"Yes. I didn't know how you like your burger, so I ordered yours plain with American cheese, like mine."

She remembered the processed cheese in his refrigerator. "Good thing I'm not lactose intolerant." She was hungry enough to eat a raw side of beef. "What'd you find out?" she asked before taking a big bite of her burger.

"Not much, unfortunately. Neither of my coworkers knows who the man is."

She stopped chewing. "Are you serious?"

"As serious as the heart attack you're going to have after eating that burger."

She set the burger down on the foil wrapper. "This isn't a joking matter, Guy. There are mean men chasing me for these photographs," she said, close to tears.

His face grew somber. "I didn't mean to upset you." He placed his arm around her shoulders and pulled her into him. "I was only trying to lighten the mood. My coworkers and I came up with a plan. We have no intention of letting those mean men get to you."

Sniffling, she pushed him away. "Stop teasing me."

He massaged her shoulder. "If you'll give me a chance, I'll explain our plan."

She inhaled an unsteady breath. "I'm sorry. I get emotional when I'm sleep deprived."

"Not to mention having your house broken into and being chased by thugs." He set his burger down and wiped his mouth. "So Rich, one of my coworkers, has a friend who might be able to help us. Problem is, the guy's a little hard to get in touch with." Guy gave her a full report of his meeting with Rich and James.

"And you're sure you gave them a cropped photograph of Brosnan and not the original one?" she asked when he finished talking.

"I'm positive." He ate the last of his burger and balled up his foil wrapper, tossing it back into the empty bag. "Honestly, though, I don't have high hopes of them finding Baird this weekend. His voice message indicated he was unreachable until Monday. You need to prepare yourself. It might take awhile to identify the mystery man."

She glared at him. "How long? I leave for Rio in less than a week."

He slumped back against the sofa cushions. "I forgot about your trip to the Olympics. Who knows how long it will take for them to get in touch with Baird? Even then, Baird may not recognize this character right away. Remember, Brosnan has virtually no online presence. And we don't even know if he's an American. It may be that Baird will have to do some digging."

"Who did you say he works for?"

"I didn't." Guy drew in a deep breath. "He's young, only a few years older than we are, but he has some big title with the FBI."

Scottie sprang up, her brow puckered. "So the FBI is in on my investigation now? Don't you think you should have checked with me first before you involved this Baird person?"

Guy stood to face her. "You involved us first, remember? Baird is our only hope. Take it or leave it."

Scottie gathered up their trash and stomped off to the kitchen while Guy poured them an after-dinner drink—Baileys and cream on the rocks.

He handed her a glass when she returned. "I can't afford to sit around and wait, Guy. My photographs are already yesterday's news. They will be obsolete by the end of the weekend."

"That's not true in this situation. As long as they go viral before November 8…"

Something on the TV behind Guy caught her attention. "I've been thinking about the situation a lot while you were gone. I have another idea that involves this." She pointed to the muted TV where CNN was running a segment about Catherine Caine's upcoming Main Street Tour. Tastefully designed, the American flag was painted on one side of the bus, and on the other—*The Caine Cruiser, Catherine Caine for President* in red, white, and blue.

Guy grabbed the remote from the coffee table and turned up the volume. They watched as the CNN correspondent took her viewers on a tour of the inside of the bus. A conference area, complete with leather recliners, occupied a portion of the front of the bus while the rear was used for the candidate's personal space—including a bed for napping, a plush lavatory, a hair and makeup station, and a closet with outfits for every occasion in every style of fabric, most designed in shades of red or blue.

Guy clicked off the TV when the segment ended. "I don't understand. How does Caine's tricked-out tour bus fit in with your predicament?"

Scottie smiled. "Because I'm the newest Caine Groupie. The senator's Main Street Tour starts tomorrow. Caine is traveling in her bus, making appearances on the main streets of small towns across the country. She's starting in the Southeast and concentrating on North Carolina and Florida with stops in Virginia, South Carolina, and Georgia. I'm going to follow her tour."

"You can't be serious." Guy stared at her, as though waiting for her to admit she was joking.

"I'm dead serious." Drink in hand, she dropped back down to the sofa. "If Brosnan and Caine are involved in a romantic relationship, he will be hanging out on the periphery of the crowd, waiting for an opportunity to hook up with her again."

"Do you realize how dangerous that could be?" He sat down beside her. "These mean men, as you call them, will be on the lookout for you. They will spot your blonde head from miles away."

"That's where you're wrong. They won't recognize me, because I'm a master when it comes to disguise."

In truth, other than Halloween and other themed parties in college, Scottie had dressed in disguise only one time—and only a few months ago. A Rastafarian wig and ratty trench coat had protected her identity when she'd been forced to return baby Mary to her biological grandparents this past Christmas.

Guy perked up. "I like the sound of that. What kind of disguises are we talking about?" he asked as a suggestive smile played on his lips.

Scottie brought a finger to her chin. "Oh... you know, the usual. I like to dress up like a nurse or waitress, sometimes a cheerleader."

Guy licked his lips. "This is sounding better and better. Maybe I should go on this road trip with you."

"Ha." Scottie threw one of the sofa pillows at him. "I don't remember inviting you."

"I'm inviting myself. You shouldn't be alone. Someone needs to protect you from the mean men."

"And you're just the cowboy to do it?"

He glanced around the room. "Looks to me like I'm the only cowboy applying for the job." Draping his arm across the back of the sofa, he turned to face her. "Seriously, Scottie, I might as well put my cards on the table. If we're going to be working together, we should be honest with one another. I'm attracted to you. I have been since we met in the Richmond airport. I've been trying to ignore these feelings as much as I can. I don't think that going on this trip with you is necessarily the best choice for me, but I can't let you go alone, not with the goon platoon chasing you."

Butterflies flitted around her stomach and her mind raced with indecent thoughts of spending time alone with him on a road-trip adventure. "I don't understand why you having feelings for me is a problem when I feel the same way."

"Because you've only been separated from your husband for a few days. I don't want to be your rebound person." He twisted a lock of her hair around his finger. "You're different from other girls I've met. I admire your passion, and your impulsive nature excites me. I'd like a chance at a meaningful relationship with you, but I don't want to compete with ghosts from your past."

"I appreciate your honesty." She sipped her drink and sat in silence, overwhelmed by her emotions. Excitement. Disappointment. Relief. She knew a romantic fling between them would cloud her judgment and sidetrack her from her goals. Finally taking in a deep breath, she said, "For me, as far as my feelings for you are concerned, I can tell you that the breakup of my marriage isn't the issue. My career is. I may never get another chance at a story like this. I can't afford the distraction right now."

"Staying focused is important to me as well."

"Okay, then. Why don't we agree to keep our relationship platonic, at least for now?"

He looked away, then turned back and gazed directly into her eyes. "All right. It won't be easy, but I think it's for the best."

"Good. Now let's get to work." Scottie scooted to the edge of the couch and flipped open her laptop. She accessed Catherine Caine's website. "Look at this itinerary." She slid the computer over to him. "The senator's schedule is brutal."

His eyes traveled the page as he scrolled down. "Some of these towns are places I've always wanted to visit." He stood and stretched. "First stop is eight o'clock tomorrow morning in Leesburg, Virginia, which is less than an hour away. Factoring in a quick shopping trip for disguises at the Wal-Mart in Tyson's Corner, assuming they are actually open 24/7 like they advertise, we should allow for two hours, which means we need to leave here at six. I need to do some laundry first, though."

He went into his bedroom and returned with a laundry basket. Scottie watched as he opened a pair of bifold louvered doors in the kitchen, which concealed a washing machine and dryer. He dumped the contents of his basket into the machine, tossed in a detergent pod, and set the controls. He opened the dryer and began folding wrinkled clothes. Impressive. Guy had done more laundry in five minutes than Scottie had seen Brad do in five years.

She drained the rest of her Baileys and rinsed her glass in the kitchen sink. "I should get going. Six o'clock will come early. Is there a decent hotel nearby?"

"You're not going anywhere alone, not with the mean men on the loose." He inclined his head toward his bedroom. "You can have my room. I'll sleep on the sofa."

"Are you holding me hostage?" An unsolicited image of him handcuffing her to his bed popped into her head. *Geez, Scottie, retract the horns.*

He beamed. "Now I like the sound of that." When she gave him a reproachful look, he added, "Sorry. I forgot about our deal. This friends only relationship isn't going to be easy."

15

SCOTTIE BARELY SLEPT. And it wasn't because she'd insisted that she sleep on the sofa, which turned out to be quite comfortable. Thoughts of Guy's sexy body sprawled out on his bed in such close proximity to her had played in her mind throughout the night. She considered breaking her own ground rules by taking off her clothes and crawling in beside him. With such lustful thoughts, she didn't know how she would survive traveling with him, but she needed to get a grip on her libido for the sake of her story. For the benefit of her career.

Around four o'clock, she gave into her sleeplessness and decided to get up and shower. The day ahead would be long and hot. But first she needed to retrieve the suitcase she'd left in her car. Back in Guy's apartment, she stayed in the shower until her fingers wrinkled and the water ran cold. She dressed quickly in knee-length black yoga pants and a gray Nike workout tank, and then went to the kitchen in search of coffee. In contrast to the meager contents of his refrigerator, the assortment of K-Cup choices was large—coffee, tea, and lattes. He even had two boxes of her personal favorite—Krispy Kreme Smooth.

"You're up early," Guy said, joining her in the kitchen. He

wore a pair of gym shorts and nothing else. His smooth muscular chest and six-pack abs nearly sent her heart into cardiac arrest.

She tried not to stare at his body, but failed. "It's five fifteen. We need to get on the road soon."

When he reached over her to get a K-Cup from the coffee cabinet, the earthy scent of his body filled the space between them. She stepped out of his way.

He set his K-Cup in the machine and lowered the handle to brew. "I hope you slept better than I did. Knowing your naked body was on the other side of the door made me have all kinds of stress dreams."

She set her coffee mug down on the counter. "First of all, I slept in my clothes, as if it's any of your business. And secondly, we aren't going to make it out of the parking deck if we don't put these feelings aside," she said, as much to herself as to him.

His eyes twinkled over the rim of his mug, as he blew on his coffee.

"I'm serious, Guy. This story is important to me. You either need to play by my rules or stay at home."

He took a sip of coffee, and then lowered his mug. "You're right. I'm way out of line. I want to be an asset to you, not a hindrance." He walked toward the bathroom. "I'll just go take a cold shower. I'm sure you didn't leave me any hot water anyway. I'll be ready to go in fifteen minutes."

He reappeared a few minutes later looking even more scrumptious in khaki shorts and burgundy polo shirt and smelling delicious, like the Old Spice man soap her brother used. Flinging his duffel bag over his shoulder, he locked the door behind them and removed her suitcase from her hand. An awkward silence filled the elevator going down. Scottie stared at the floor, doing her best to avoid looking at his muscular calves. She followed him through the lobby and into the garage.

"Where'd you park?" he asked.

"Second level," she said and led him down the stairs.

He stopped dead in his tracks when her yellow Mini came into view. "Damn. I forgot all about your Matchbox. We can't go on a road trip in a toy car." He leaned down and peered inside the Mini. I can't fit one of my legs inside that passenger compartment, let alone my big feet."

Scottie popped the hatch and took her suitcase from him, tossing it inside. "Since you don't have a car, I guess you'll have to stay here." She slammed the rear door shut.

"Hold on." He grabbed her by the arm before she could get in the car. "We can figure something out. Let me call a friend of mine who owes me a favor."

Scottie tapped on her watch. "You have five minutes, Guy. I'm not going to miss the first event because of you."

Guy walked twenty feet away from her and placed his call. He returned, grinning. "Robbie is not very happy with me for waking him up at six o'clock on a Saturday morning, but he says we can use his car. Can I trust you to wait for me here while I run up and get his keys?"

She sat down on the rear bumper. "As long as you hurry."

True to his word, Guy was back in a flash. And, although she would never admit it to him, Scottie thought Robbie's Jeep with its leather seats and satellite radio was a much better option for extended road travel. Cruising through the light morning traffic, they made it to Tyson's Corner in no time.

"Let's divide and conquer," she said. They entered the store and she headed toward the women's department.

"Wait a minute, Scottie," he called after her. "I don't know what I'm supposed to buy."

"Anything that will turn you into somebody you're not," she

said over her shoulder. "I'll meet you at the checkout counter in fifteen minutes."

Scottie picked out hats in different shapes and sizes, an assortment of sunglasses, and bandannas in a variety of colors. When they reconvened at the checkout counter, Guy's basket was overflowing and his smile was wide. "That was fun. I like this game." He held up a black leather biker's vest. "This is a good look for me, don't you think?"

"OMG, I've created a monster." She rolled her eyes, although secretly his enthusiasm pleased her.

He offered his credit card, but she insisted on paying the bill. "It's worth whatever I have to pay to see you in that wife beater," she said, eying the black tank top on the counter.

He placed his hand on his chest in mock horror. "If I didn't know any better, I'd think you were flirting with me. Which is entirely against our friends without benefits rules."

*

Scottie waited until they were on the road to Leesburg before she asked Guy why he didn't own a car. "I mean, it's really none of my business. Please tell me, you haven't been arrested for drunk driving or anything like that."

He chuckled. "How long have you been sitting on that question?"

She shrugged. "I'm just making conversation."

He thought about it for twenty seconds. "I don't know, truthfully. I just never got around to buying one, I guess. I had a fleet of trucks and four-wheel drives at my disposal back on the farm. I never saw the need to own a car at Chapel Hill. I always flew home to see my family. And now, since I ride the Metro or take Uber, I don't see the point in paying expensive garage fees in DC."

"That makes sense, I guess."

"Not much of a story there for the investigative journalist."

"Sorry." She turned away, looking out the window. "I didn't realize our arrangement prohibited us from getting to know one another."

"Lighten up, Scottie. I'm just teasing."

Settling in to silence, they listened to Guy's country music playlist the rest of the way to Leesburg.

"What disguise are you wearing for our first event?" Guy asked when they were five miles outside of town.

"We're going to a political rally, Guy, not a Halloween party," she said, cringing at the sound of her harsh tone. She couldn't explain why she'd all of a sudden turned into a bitch, especially when she knew he was teasing her. Frustration at being able to look but not touch. Irritation at having to sit on the story of the decade while she traveled all over Virginia and North Carolina verifying the facts.

The last thing she wanted was for their relationship to be hostile. If she couldn't snap out of her snarky mood, they would both be in for a long trip. "I think we need to keep it simple this first time around." Rummaging around in her Wal-Mart bag, she slipped a cubic zirconia engagement ring on her finger. "What do you think?" She ran her hands down her workout clothes. "Do I pass for a wealthy wife on her way to yoga class?"

He gestured at the shopping bag on the floorboard. "All that stuff you bought, and that's the best you can do?"

"You won't fit in at this event wearing that Harley vest, I'm sorry to say. We're going to Loudon County, horse country, where the mean income is over a million dollars a year. Most of that is made from dividends earned from stock portfolios of the extremely wealthy." She eyed his khaki shorts and polo shirt. "You're dressed just right to be my husband."

"Your husband, huh? I hope the promotion comes with perks, if you know what I mean," he said, wiggling his eyebrows.

She couldn't help but laugh at his ridiculous expression. "Don't get any ideas, wise guy. You are only my *pretend* husband."

He stuck out his lower lip in a pout. "If you say so."

"Will you be serious?"

He sat up straighter in his seat. "I am being serious when I tell you to do something with your hair. You'll stand out in the crowd with all those blonde curls."

"Fine," she said, knotting her blonde mane in a loose bun on the top of her head.

They arrived in Leesburg and drove around the small downtown area until they located the Caine Cruiser. Guy parallel parked on the same street two blocks away. Scottie retrieved her purse from the backseat, but left her electronics bag hidden under her Wal-Mart bag on the floorboard.

"You're not taking your camera?" Guy asked.

"Not this time. The camera would spoil my disguise. I can't very well wear my press pass with my yoga clothes, and my professional lens screams reporter. We need to use our eyes and ears while we're getting the lay of the land."

"Then it's a good thing I brought my binoculars." He produced a pair of Swarovski binoculars from the center console."

"Whoa. Now those are cool." She snatched the binoculars away from him and held them to her eyes. "Good grief. I can see the veins on that man's bulbous nose three blocks away. They're every bit as clear as my L glass. Is this what you use for cattle driving?" She returned the binoculars to him.

"And bird watching."

"Are you willing to share them?"

"Sure." He dropped the binoculars into her handbag. "In fact, it'll be a little less conspicuous if you keep them."

Event planners had cordoned off three blocks of King Street where local businesses had organized, for the citizens of Leesburg and surrounding areas, a Saturday Sunrise Social—which included an opportunity to meet and greet the candidate. At one end of the street, a fresh market, set up by merchants and farmers, featured wooden trolleys overflowing with locally grown fruits and vegetables, and tented booths carrying specialty items—Virginia peanuts and wines, as well as jams and jellies and honey. At the other end of the block, restaurant owners were offering generous portions of their most popular breakfast items—mini quiches, pastries, and ham biscuits. Banquet tables with red-checkered tablecloths and white folding chairs occupied the center of the block, giving those gathered an opportunity to greet their neighbor or meet a new friend.

A long line of people waited at the coffee kiosk for their choice of freshly ground coffee grown from all around the world. Once they had coffee in hand, his from Ethiopia and hers from Colombia, Scottie and Guy found an out-of-the-way spot to survey the crowd.

"Look, there's the senator." Scottie inclined her head at a cluster of people laughing and talking on the opposite side of the street. Two Secret Service agents stood to attention on either side of the candidate, their eyes darting about as they scanned the crowd. They were not the same agents as the two she'd seen in the alley. She recognized the woman standing behind the senator as the same young woman who had followed Caine when she exited the convention center that night in Philadelphia.

"I'm going to meet her," Scottie said.

Guy cut his eyes at Scottie. "You're kidding, right? Her people will recognize you right away."

"I don't think so. I was wearing dark clothes that night.

16

AKING GUY PROMISE not to look, Scottie climbed into the backseat on the way to Charlottesville and ...ed into denim shorts and a pale-blue tank. She wore the ...clothes but changed her hat for the next two events, choos-...rst a floppy straw hat and then an Atlanta Braves baseball ...Guy swapped out his polo shirt for a Rolling Stones tongue ...ps T-shirt, a leftover from his high school days if the yellow ...its were any indication.

...Much like the Sunrise Social, city executives blocked off ...of downtown for each of the remainder events on Saturday, ...g the candidate an opportunity to mingle with pedestrians. ...r functions were more like political rallies with local politi-...speaking on behalf of the Democratic Party as well as the ...dential candidate. Although her wording often varied, ...ed to fit the needs of each particular town, the fundamen-...f the candidate's speech were the same at every stop. She ...d her position on issues like abortion and same-sex mar-...touched on her record in the Senate, expressed her concern ...the recent terrorist attacks in the country, and expounded ...bjects such as immigration, the state of the economy, and

Besides, those aren't the same Secret Service agents from the convention."

"If they know where you live, they know what you look like," he said.

"Maybe. Maybe not." Scottie knew she was flirting with danger, but her investigation depended on her exploring every avenue. Whether or not she unearthed any clues, Scottie had a strong feeling that making Catherine Caine's acquaintance would one day pay off. "Who knows? If I make a lasting impression, she might offer me a job as the White House press secretary when she's elected president."

"*When* she's elected president," he scoffed. "I thought our goal was to expose her affair with Brosnan so she's *not* elected president."

"Careful, Guy. You're starting to sound like a Republican." Strolling off in the direction of the candidate, she called to him over her shoulder, "Wait here. I'll be right back."

She kept an eye on the Secret Service agents while she waited her turn to speak to Catherine Caine. Both men gave her the once over, as they did everyone who approached the senator, but neither man gave her a second look.

As for the woman who stuck close to Caine, she barely glanced in her direction.

When the group ahead of her walked away, Scottie stepped up to the senator and offered her hand. "I'm Mary Scott Westport, and I'm honored to meet you. I'm impressed with your record in the Senate as well as your honest concern for the American people."

"I hope that means I can count on your support in November," Caine said.

"I'm considering it, yes. But voting for you would make me the first to vote outside of the Republican Party in my family's history." Scottie leaned into the candidate. "You won't tell my father now, will you?"

At the exact moment Catherine Caine tilted her head back and laughed, the woman standing behind Scottie—who was inappropriately dressed for her age and for the time of day—stumbled on her four-inch heels and fell into Scottie, sending Scottie's coffee down the front of Caine's blue silk sheath.

The Secret Service agents closed in around them. When Scottie saw the damage to Caine's dress, tears welled in her eyes and her hand flew to her mouth. "I'm so sorry. And embarrassed."

Alerted to the disaster, the crowd around her gasped and mumbled disapproval, making Scottie feel even worse.

The young woman with Caine rushed to her side with a handful of napkins, and began to blot the stain on the senator's dress.

"Don't worry, Mary Scott. It wasn't your fault at all. These things happen all the time." Caine lifted the silk fabric away from her body while the blotting continued. "The coffee is a little warm though."

"Thank you for being so understanding," Scottie said. "I don't imagine Andrew Blackmore would be so gracious."

Caine tilted her head back and laughed. "You're probably right. But don't tell him I said so." Then Caine turned to the young woman and said, "Thank you, Lucy. That's fine for now."

"I'd be happy to pay for your dry cleaning," Scottie offered.

"No need. I have two more dresses just like this one on the Cruiser for situations like these."

"Okay, then. I won't take up anymore of your time," Scottie said. "I'm sorry we met under these circumstances, but your kindness has earned you another fifty points in my polls."

"Well then, it was coffee well spilt," Caine said.

"I'd love to help out on your campa[...] about doing that?"

"Wonderful. We are always looking [...] teers such as yourself." Caine motioned [...] this is Mary Scott Westport. She's intere[...] campaign."

Lucy keyed Scottie's name into her ce[...] business card in her hand. "I'll have some [...]

Scottie studied the card as she fough[...] the crowd.

"That was some last impression you [...] ing his head in amazement. "Only you [...] down a senator's dress and walk away [...] in hand."

"Don't get too excited," Scottie said [...] card in her purse. "These numbers are gen[...] have gotten myself from the Internet."

foreign affairs. Scottie grew to like the senator more and more with every mile they traveled.

In Virginia, the charming townsfolk of Charlottesville and Lexington set up hot dog and ice cream stands, and brought in magicians and puppeteers for the children's entertainment. Charlottesville hosted a pie baking contest with the honorable senator as the judge. Lexington organized a kick-off parade with gleaming fire engines, antique cars, and magnificent show horses decked out in all their glory. And Roanoke, the final stop of the day, brought in a popular local bluegrass band and provided BBQ, slaw, and all the fixings from local vendors.

Catherine Caine spent time with every person she met. She kissed babies, shook the hands of old people whose fingers and knuckles were gnarled with arthritis, and discussed agriculture with scruffy-bearded farmers dressed in overalls.

After what Scottie deemed a successful mission in Leesburg, she felt comfortable wearing her press pass for the rest of the day's events. She and Guy approached their search for Brosnan in an organized manner. They'd separate the crowd of attendees into sections and scrutinize every face through a magnifying glass—his binoculars as well as her camera fitted with the largest zoom lens.

When the bluegrass band strummed the last chord on the banjo, signifying the end of a very long day, the senator's team swept her away to the Caine Cruiser. But an hour later, the tour bus was still idling across the parking lot from where Scottie and Guy sat waiting.

"I wish they'd make a move already," Guy said, watching the Cruiser with his binoculars. "If I have to drive to North Carolina tonight, I'd like to get on the highway."

They didn't have access to the senator's personal itinerary, but the schedule posted on her website indicated Caine would attend services the following morning at eleven o'clock at St Paul's Church in Asheville, North Carolina. Everything else, such as highway routes and hotels, was all top secret.

Scottie had spent the past fifteen minutes scrutinizing her images of Caine and Brosnan. "Look at these photographs closely, Guy." She handed him her iPad. "I'm not convinced these two are romantically involved. Look at the kiss, just off to the side of her lips." She swiped her finger across the iPad as she scrolled through the images. "And the way he holds her at arm's length when he embraces her. Who's to say this wasn't an innocent encounter? My brother, Will, suggested that this man is just a big donor who prefers to remain anonymous. I'm starting to think he might be right."

"I'm not seeing it, Scottie. There's no doubt in my mind these two are lovers." He handed her back the iPad. "You're buying too much into the bullshit Caine is preaching. Don't go getting soft on me."

"I'll admit I like her message, but it's more than that. She handled the whole coffee incident with the grace of a truly nice person, not some unscrupulous woman who cheats on her husband."

"Give me a break. She's a politician. She understands all too well how copping attitudes costs votes."

"Spoken like a true campaign worker." She dropped the iPad in her bag on the floor. "You've been driving all day. Let me drive for a change."

Before Guy could argue with her, Scottie got out of the car and went around to the driver's side, the sundress she'd changed into billowing out behind her.

"I am kind of tired," he admitted. He climbed out of the car and stretched his long limbs. "I'll take a little nap, then we can switch somewhere along the way."

Guy had no sooner gotten back in the car when the tour bus pulled slowly out of the parking lot. Scottie had every intention of driving the entire four hours to Asheville, but her eyes grew heavy just the other side of Johnson City, Tennessee. She turned up the volume on the music and sipped on her Diet Coke, but nothing she tried helped her to stay awake.

She nudged Guy. "I'm sorry, Guy. I just can't stay awake. If you're not up for driving, we can find a hotel somewhere."

"I'm fine to drive," he said, returning his seat to an upright position. "Pull over at the next exit."

Scottie was sound asleep by the time they got back on the highway. She didn't stir when they arrived at the Mountain Park Inn, and slept the whole time Guy was inside talking to the night desk clerk. She bolted upright when he slammed the door upon his return.

"Where are we?" she asked, looking around confused.

"Asheville. At the Mountain Park Inn."

"Did we lose the senator?"

"No. I imagine she's inside sleeping, counting sheep as we speak. Her driver dropped Caine and all of her staff off at the front of the hotel, and then drove around back to park. At least I assume that's where he went."

"I don't care how much it cost to stay here. I can't wait to crawl into a real bed." Scottie made a move to get out of the car, but Guy grabbed her by the arm, holding her back. "I hate to tell you this, sleeping beauty,"—he brushed a stray strand of hair out of Scottie's face—"but there are no available rooms at the inn."

"That's not good. Are there other hotels close by?"

He tilted his head back against the seat and closed his eyes. "A bunch of them, but according to the desk clerk, they are sold out as well. There are a lot of people here for Caine's rally tomorrow, but there is also a big wine and food festival in town." He continued, without opening his eyes, "Did I ever tell you about the cross-country road trip I made the summer after I graduated from Chapel Hill?"

"No. I've always wanted to do something like that, but I would need to take at least a year off to photograph my way across the country. Did you start out in Wyoming?"

"Yep. I traveled the southern part of the country heading east and the northern half going west. I ended up in Washington State, and then drove all the way down to the tip of California before going home. There were times when I had nowhere to stay—for any number of reasons. Sometimes I was just too damn tired to go any farther, so I'd pull into the nearest parking lot and sleep for a few hours in the back of my Explorer."

Scottie cast a doubtful glance at the backseat. "How is that even possible considering your height?"

"You'd be surprised. Putting the seat down makes for a nice bed."

"And you're suggesting we sleep in the car tonight." Her heart skipped a beat at the thought of lying next to him in such close proximity.

He sat up and rubbed his eyes. "It doesn't appear we have any other choice. But we can't stay here." He started the engine and drove around the side of the hotel to the employee parking lot adjacent to the spa. He found an empty space and backed in between a Suburban and a minivan. He got out of the car, opened the back door, and pulled a lever that folded the rear seat flat. He stuck his head in the car. "Come on, Scottie. I promise I won't bite."

"But we don't even have any pillows or blankets."

"We can use the clothes from our suitcases."

Scottie got out and shuffled around to the back of the SUV.

She unzipped her suitcase and removed several T-shirts, rolling them up into a neck pillow. "Brrr... It's cold out here."

"You're in the mountains, sweetheart. Do you want to borrow my jacket?" He plucked a windbreaker out of his duffel bag.

"No thanks. I have a sweatshirt." She tugged her favorite one of Brad's old UVA sweatshirts over her head. The worn article of clothing was like a baby blanket to her. When she kicked him out, she couldn't bring herself to pack the sweatshirt with the rest of his things. Was it wrong of her to sleep next to another man while wearing her husband's sweatshirt, even if he was her soon-to-be ex-husband? Scottie mentally slapped herself. *Brad slept with another woman, you fool.* She heard Will's voice in her right ear, like the devil sitting on one shoulder. *Be free, little birdie. Spread your wings and fly.* Then in her left ear, she heard Guy whispering, *I don't want to compete with ghosts from your past.*

"Well, what are we waiting for?" Guy waved his hand at the SUV, gesturing for her to get in. She climbed in the back and he crawled in beside her, closing the rear door behind him. He cuddled up to her, spooning her, his tight abs and muscular thighs pressing against her. He tickled her neck with his nose. "Mmm. I could get used to this."

"You're crossing the line, Guy."

He wrapped his arm around her. "I'm protecting you against ax murderers."

The idea of him protecting her appealed to Scottie. Everything about him appealed to her. Five more minutes in this position and she wouldn't be able to control herself. *You can't afford the distraction, Scottie.*

She elbowed him in the ribs. "I'm serious, Guy. If you don't face the other way, I'm going to drag my suitcase up here between us."

"All right," he said, groaning as he rolled over. "But if you change your mind, don't hesitate to wake me, no matter the time."

She lay next to him for hours, unable to sleep, thinking of all the things she wanted him to do to her. She finally drifted off, and woke again as the sky was turning pink over the mountains. Rolling over on her side, she propped herself up on one elbow and watched Guy sleep. His breathing was soft, and every now and then, a smile tugged at the corners of his lips. He moaned, and Scottie hoped he was dreaming of her. The scent of man soap had long since worn off, and his body smelled of last night's dinner—barbecue and vanilla ice cream cones.

Anyone who sleeps so peacefully must have a clean conscience, she thought.

His eyes opened suddenly. "I see you decided to wake me after all." He cupped the back of her head and pulled her lips to his. He rolled on top of her, and his tongue parted her lips. For a brief moment she was totally lost to him. He was struggling to take off her sweatshirt when a man's face appeared in the window. Scottie caught a glimpse of a khaki uniform. The security guard. Of course.

"Hey!" The man banged on the back window. "What're you doing in there? You can't sleep here."

Guy fumbled in his pocket for the car keys. "Hold tight. This might get rough." He scrambled into the driver's seat. "The last thing we need is the police on our trail."

17

GUY SPED OUT of the parking lot and flew through the downtown streets of Asheville, blowing through yellow lights and circling blocks.

After several miles, Scottie climbed over the seats and slid in next to Guy on the passenger side. "You can slow down you. The security guard isn't following us. He didn't even get in his car."

"Don't burst my bubble. This might be the closest I ever get to being Jason Bourne. I'm sure he got our license plate number. More than likely he called the police."

"And what, reported us for sleeping in our car on hotel grounds? The Mountain Park Inn isn't exactly private property."

"If it was private property, we'd be considered trespassing. In this case, we were just loitering." They stopped at a red light and he eyed the cars parked in the lot of a nearby shopping center. "Maybe we should steal a license plate."

"I'm sure your friend would love that."

"He'll never know. We can screw the stolen plates on top of Robbie's, then take them off when we leave town."

"Please, Guy. Enough with the cloak and dagger stuff. All I want to do right now is brush my teeth."

"I can arrange that." He drove around town until he found an old Exxon station with single restrooms on the back. They filled up with gas, and then went inside for the keys to the restrooms.

Taking a change of clothes and her cosmetic case from her suitcase, Scottie went into the women's room and locked the door. She stripped naked except for her flip-flops. She brushed her teeth first, then squirted liquid soap on a handful of brown paper towels and washed the parts of her body that needed it the most. She splashed water over her body to rinse the soap away, and patted her arms and legs dry with more paper towels. She washed her hair as best she could in the tiny sink, then stuck her head under the hand dryer to get some of the moisture out. After fashioning her hair in a single braid down her back, she slipped on a pair of white shorts and a Dave Matthews T-shirt. A bucket hat pulled down over her head completed her look.

Guy was waiting for her in the car with hot coffee and Krispy Kreme doughnuts from the kiosk inside.

"What're we gonna do all morning?" she asked. "The first event doesn't start for hours."

"I thought you were planning to go to the church service with the senator?"

Scottie glanced down at her clothing. "I'm hardly dressed for a high Episcopal service." She removed a chocolate-iced doughnut from the bag. "We can't go back to the Mountain Park Inn, not with Barney Fife on the lookout for us. I could be missing my big opportunity. Caine and Brosnan are probably having kinky sex in the penthouse suite as we speak. Not that I actually believe that, but you get the point."

He bit into a jelly doughnut. "Maybe we were too ambitious in assuming we could maintain round-the-clock surveillance on Caine."

"The chances of me getting another photograph of them in a compromising position are not high. I'm beginning to think this whole plan is stupid, another one of my impulse decisions that either leads to trouble or never works out."

"Hey, now, where's the Scottie spirit?" he asked, wiping the glaze off her mouth with his napkin. "Besides, I thought the point was to identify the mystery man. You already have the photographs you need."

"True, but more compromising photographs would seal the deal. But I can't do either if I can't find him."

"You're just tired, Scottie, and understandably so. You've covered two political conventions, broken up with your husband, and had your house ransacked, all within a matter of two weeks. You need to save something in your tank for the Olympics."

She agreed with him, but she was too stubborn to admit it. "I can sleep on the flight to Rio."

He eyed her suspiciously. "You're not planning to follow this convoy until then, are you?"

"Yep. As long as it takes for Brosnan to show up."

"There is more than one way to break the story, Scottie. I'm sure I don't need to tell you that. You're the journalist. But if things don't work out on this Main Street Tour, or whatever they're calling it"—he waved his jelly doughnut through the air—"the story will keep until you get back from the Olympics. Hell, it might even take Rich that long to get in touch with Baird."

Scottie eyed him with suspicion. He sounded like he wanted out. And after only one night on the road. She had not taken him for a quitter. "What exactly are you trying to say, Guy? If you want to give up and go home, feel free to do so. I'm perfectly fine on my own. You probably have to get back to work tomorrow anyway."

"I'm not worried about work. I have some vacation time coming to me. All I'm saying is you should consider setting some parameters for your investigation."

"Like what?" she asked, peering at him over the rim of her coffee cup.

"Let me see the itinerary."

She accessed Caine's website and held the iPad out for him to see. "We eat lunch in Asheville and an early dinner in Hillsborough before we head to the beach."

"I'm all for digging my toes in the sand." He took the iPad from her and scrolled down. "Good lord. She has four different stops scheduled up and down the coast tomorrow with the grand finale at the seafood festival in Beaufort tomorrow night." He closed the cover on the iPad and handed it back to her. "If I were you, I'd stay with the tour until Tuesday morning when the Cruiser heads inland to Raleigh. If Brosnan hasn't shown up by then, I would consider my other options."

Scottie rolled her eyes. "Because I have so many of them."

"You have one good option, and a handful of others worth considering. Submitting your images to your most trusted news associate and letting them identify the mystery man seems like the most logical solution. That way, you at least get half credit."

"Half credit isn't good enough in this case. What are the other options worth considering?"

"Saying to hell with it and throwing the images up on Twitter and Facebook."

"That's irresponsible journalism, Guy, and I will have no part of it."

He wadded up the doughnut bag and tossed it in the back-seat. "I'm on your side here. I was simply trying to get you to understand your options." Shifting in his seat to face her, he tilted her chin up toward him. "Let's forget about Catherine Caine for a minute and talk about that kiss."

"There you go crossing the line again."

"Now that we both have clean breath, I think we should try it again, to see if it was as good as I remember."

She bit down on her lip to hide her smile. Although she would never admit it to him, she was enjoying their flirtation. His kiss had stirred parts of her body she thought were dead. But she needed to remain focused. Taking her eye off the prize could cost her the story. "Despite what *you* think, *I* think we should establish some parameters on our relationship, whereby you keep your hands to yourself until this investigation is over."

"Where's the fun in that?"

He parted his lips to kiss her, but she pushed him away. "If you're a good boy, maybe I'll let you kiss me again when we get to the beach. But just a kiss, nothing more."

His eyes lit up. "I'll take whatever I can get."

*

The rest of the day proved problematic for Scottie and Guy. When her favorite lens jammed, Scottie spent most of the gourmet picnic at Pack Square Park seeking advice from other photographers. Then, Robbie's SUV wouldn't start as they were preparing to leave Asheville for the rally in Hillsborough. Lucky for them, an older gentleman, parked two rows over in the parking lot, had a pair of jumper cables in his pickup truck.

"It's the heat," the man said, once the SUV was running. "If I were you, I'd stop by a garage and have them test the battery. It's just gonna happen again if your battery is outta juice."

Guy and Scottie missed most of the rally by the time they located a Firestone, switched out the battery, and made the four-hour drive to Hillsborough. Nibbling on shriveled-up hot dogs and burned baked beans, they observed the crowd while listening to the end of Caine's rah-rah speech. They got back in the car for another four-hour drive to the beach, only to get a speeding ticket along the way.

Scottie sensed Guy's patience diminishing as the evening wore on. But instead of complaining about the long hours in the car—or the fine he would have to pay and the points he would receive on his license for driving ten miles over the speed limit—Guy turned silent, preferring loud music over the light chatter they had carried on for most of the trip.

A few minutes before eleven that night, they crossed the causeway into Atlantic Beach, took a right-hand turn on West Fort Macon Road, and drove for miles until they came to a residential area known as Pine Knoll Shores.

"No matter the cost, they better have a room available wherever Caine is staying," Scottie said.

"I wouldn't get my hopes up if I were you," Guy said as the Caine Cruiser pulled into the driveway of an oceanfront beach cottage. "Looks like she's rented a house." He turned into the public beach access two lots over. "What do we do now?"

"We passed a few hotels a while back. Why don't you call them while I sneak down the road for a peek?" Scottie grabbed his binoculars from the center console and hopped out of the car.

She made her way back to the road, and then walked down to the house where the Cruiser was parked. Hiding in the hedgerow of the house next door, she spied on the senator's staff as they removed suitcases and supplies from the cargo hold of the tour bus. The beach house was lit up like the White House. Counting the windows on the second and third floors, Scottie estimated the cedar shake *cottage* had at least eleven bedrooms, enough to accommodate the entire team.

Scottie hurried back to the car, and slipped into the passenger seat. "Looks like the senator's whole team is staying at the beach house. Did you have any luck finding a hotel nearby?"

Guy shook his head. "The Hampton Inn and Double Tree are both full."

"What? On a Sunday night?"

He shrugged. "Apparently there's a big fishing tournament over in Morehead City. All the better hotels in the area are sold out. I'd rather camp on the beach than stay in the other dumpy-looking beach motels."

Scottie considered the idea. "We passed a Wal-Mart on the way in. We could go back for supplies to make our campout more enjoyable," she said, mustering enthusiasm she didn't feel.

He nodded, his mouth set in a firm line. "Wal-Mart it is, then."

18

AN AWKWARD SILENCE fell over them as they headed back toward the causeway. Scottie suspected Guy would abandon their cause in the morning, twenty-four hours earlier than the cutoff date she'd set at his insistence. She didn't blame him. She'd pack up and go home with him if she could. Nothing had gone their way all day, and she was beginning to doubt Pierce Brosnan would show up at all. She only hoped the story would keep until she returned from Rio.

She felt a pang in her chest when she realized she might never see Guy again.

All the more reason to make the night memorable.

Guy found a spot close to the entrance to Wal-Mart in the nearly empty parking lot. "Divide and conquer, same as last time?" Scottie asked, once they were inside the store.

"Fine," he said in a clipped tone.

"I'll go to the bed and bath section if you'll grab some bottled water and a few snacks." They each grabbed a cart and took off in opposite directions.

Scottie spared no expense on the items she selected. Might as well have the best comfort money could buy at Wal-Mart, considering she was saving hundreds of dollars on hotel rooms. She filled her basket with plush throw blankets and feather pillows, thick bath sheets and washcloths. She went to the hardware section and bought two battery-operated lanterns and citronella candle buckets to fight off the bugs. In the grocery section, she found a roll of toilet paper and a bottle of liquid bath soap. When she caught up with Guy, he was already in line at the checkout. In addition to the bags of Doritos and Cheetos and a box of Frosted Strawberry Pop-Tarts, he placed an Igloo cooler and a large bag of ice on the conveyer—needed to cool down the twelve-pack of Corona Light, bottle of Chardonnay, case of Dasani water, and individual-size bottles of Simply Orange juice in his cart.

I have to introduce this guy to Will, she thought. *If his eating habits are any indication, they will be fast friends.*

Guy ripped into the carton of Corona as soon as they got back to the car. Using the bottle opener on Robbie's key chain, he popped the cap off and drained half the bottle. Dropping the bag of ice on the pavement to break up the chunks, he loaded the Igloo with drinks and spread the ice on top.

"Here." He tossed her the car keys. "Do you mind driving?" Guy removed another Corona from the cooler before slamming the rear door shut.

The silence continued on the way back to the beach access lot. Guy finished his first beer, and then guzzled most of his second. When they arrived, he hopped out of the SUV. "If you can get the bag of snacks, I'll head down to the beach with the cooler."

Since she first met him in the airport parking lot, Guy had gone out of his way to be helpful to her, but this behavior bordered on rudeness. She replayed the events of the day in her mind, trying to pinpoint the moment when things between them had turned sour.

Scottie took her time gathering her purchases, hoping to give

Guy the opportunity to process whatever it was that was irritating him. Fifteen minutes later, her arms loaded with supplies, she made her way down to the beach.

Guy jumped up to help her. "I didn't realize you had so much stuff."

Scottie noticed two empty beer bottles on the sand beside the cooler, the reason for the sudden change in his mood.

He took the blanket from her and spread it out on the beach. "I'm sorry, but the wine is still pretty warm."

"Then I'll have a beer." She stretched out on the blanket, staring up at the full moon lighting up the night sky. "What a beautiful night. We certainly don't need the lanterns with the moon so bright."

He handed her a beer and sat down beside her.

"Looks like all the stars are present and accounted for. Does the night sky look the same in Wyoming?"

He tilted his head back, studying the stars. "I guess so. I've never really thought about it."

Scottie closed her eyes and listened to the ocean roar. "When we were little, my family rented the same cottage every year in the Outer Banks just north of here. The house didn't have air-conditioning, so we kept the windows and doors open all the time. When we returned home from our vacation, I had to adjust to the quiet on our farm without the sound of the waves crashing on the sand." Sitting up, she wrapped her arms around her knees. "I've always wondered what people who live in landlocked states do for their annual vacation. Did your family take a trip to the beach every summer, or did you go hiking or white water rafting or something mountainy like that?"

"My parents took us to Huntington Beach in Southern California when I was twelve, and I went to Mexico on my senior class trip when I graduated from high school. But those were the only two times I'd been to the beach until I moved to DC. Now I try to go at least once a summer. I love the water."

Guy opened a bag of Doritos and stuffed a handful of chips into his mouth. He offered her the bag.

She waved him away. "No thanks."

"Cheetos?" he asked, reaching for the bag.

She shook her head. "I try not to eat too much of that stuff."

He hung his head, looking like a guilty puppy. "I should've asked you what kind of snacks you wanted."

"I'm not hungry now, but I'll be excited for Pop-Tarts in the morning."

He yanked on her braid. "I apologize for my bad mood earlier. The speeding ticket really put a damper on my day."

She nudged him. "I don't blame you if you want to call it quits. The past two days have been anything but easy. You can drop me at the nearest car rental place in the morning and be back in DC by early afternoon."

"No way. I intend to honor the parameters we agreed upon. If Brosnan hasn't shown up by Tuesday morning, we'll decide on a different plan together." He looked away from her. "I'm not in the mood tonight, but tomorrow, you and I need to talk about my job."

"Unless you're a hired assassin, I don't see why it matters how you make a living."

"Trust me," he mumbled. "In this situation, it matters."

Not wanting to spoil their reestablished conviviality, she let the subject drop. For the next hour, they sipped beer, dug their toes in the sand, and limited their conversation to subjects that had nothing to do with their careers, Catherine Caine, or the upcoming election.

Guy stumbled to his feet, pulling Scottie with him. "Stand here," he said, positioning her beside the blanket. He walked two feet away, and using a shell, he drew a line in the sand between them. He took a giant step across the line. "There. Now. I've officially crossed the line, and I have no intention of going back." He leaned down and kissed her tentatively at first, then with more urgency.

"Bring it on," she whispered, breathless.

He pulled her T-shirt over her head and unclasped her bra, letting it fall to the sand. He lowered himself to the blanket, taking her with him. By the light of the moon, they explored and discovered, teased and tormented. The anticipation was like none Scottie had ever experienced, and when they finally came together, the passion took her body to heights she had no idea existed.

Afterward, they lay together, spent, under the starry night sky. She ran her fingers across his naked chest. "With those kinds of talents, why hasn't anyone dragged you down the aisle?"

He pulled the second blanket over them. "I came close once, with a girl I met in college. She ruined it for me with all the others."

"What happened?"

He rolled on his side and propped himself up on his elbow, looking down on her. "I never had a serious girlfriend before Sarah. I was always too busy working at the ranch or playing sports or practicing my guitar."

"That's interesting. I never would have taken you for a musician."

"Believe it or not, I actually belonged to a couple different bands. I fancied myself a modern-day Eric Clapton. But Sarah ruined that for me too."

"Bitch."

His gray eyes turned cloudy. "You got that right."

"I understand if you don't want to talk about it."

"I want to tell you. I don't want to hold anything back from you." Guy rolled onto his back and stared up at the sky. "I belonged to this band at UNC, a classic rock group. Mostly we played at fraternity parties, but we had our sights set on fame and glory. We were gonna be the new millennium's equivalent to the Rolling Stones. Then Sarah started sleeping with the lead singer, who at the time was one of my best friends."

"That's brutal, Guy. I'm so sorry." Scottie curled up next to him, offering the warmth of her body for comfort.

"Thanks." He wrapped his arm around her, hugging her tight. "I learned something from that painful episode, just like all the other challenges I've faced or heartaches I've experienced in my life. If not for Sarah, I'd be just another wannabe musician, traveling around the country, getting drunk every night while playing music in smoky bars. I believe that most things happen for a reason." He ran his fingers up and down her arm. "I sense that may be the case for you with the breakup of your marriage."

Her eyes filled with tears and she looked away.

"I'm sorry. I didn't mean to pry."

"You're fine." She dabbed at her eyes with the corner of the blanket. "And I agree with you that most things happen for a reason. Like Sarah, Brad did me a favor by sleeping with another woman. But the breakup of my marriage isn't the thing that's caused me the most heartache. And I've yet to decide what reason this thing happened for."

"I'm a good listener if you want to talk about it."

Scottie turned on her side, facing away from him. She didn't want to see the disappointment in his eyes when she told him about Mary. "A year ago this past March, I had a late-term miscarriage that changed my perspective on life."

"I'm sorry for your loss," he whispered in her ear.

"I appreciate that. It was a difficult time for me. After the death of my child, my desperation to have a baby consumed me, so much so that I committed a crime that would have sent me to prison if I'd been caught."

Guy kissed her neck, signaling to her that he was listening.

"Last Christmas, I was photographing a group of homeless people in Monroe Park, in downtown Richmond, for a gallery opening I was working on, when I stumbled upon a woman's dead body. Lying next to the woman, in her cardboard tent, was her four-month old child. I freaked out, of course, and called out for help, but my homeless friends took off running."

"To avoid the police."

"Exactly. I couldn't call 911, because I'd accidentally left my cell phone at home. Thinking only of getting her somewhere safe and warm until the authorities could identify the body and notify the next of kin, I picked the baby up and brought her home with me. To make a very long story short, over the course of the next few days, I bonded with the baby in a way that clouded my judgment. I convinced myself the baby was better off with me, even when her grandparents were located. I was preparing to leave town, to lead a life on the run in order to keep the baby, when my brother saved me from myself."

"Will?"

Scottie turned to face him. "How did you know his name?"

He outlined her lips with his fingertip. "You talk about him all the time, so much so you don't even realize you're talking about him."

"Will and I are close. I think the two of you would get along well. I hope someday you get a chance to meet."

"What did Will do to save you from yourself?"

"He came up with a way for me to return the baby to her grandparents and avoid the police."

"So the police knew of your involvement?"

"Sort of. They got a tip about a camera lady who frequented the park, but they never figured out that I was the camera lady."

"I can't imagine how difficult it was for you to give the baby up. Have you kept in touch with the grandparents?"

"No. They were grateful to me for taking care of their grand-daughter, but I don't think they trusted me enough to let me be a part of Mary's life. Honestly, I'm not sure it would've been good for me either. I needed to make a clean break."

"What was Brad's position on all of this?"

"He was out of town visiting family when I discovered the baby. He refused to support me when he found out about Mary. He walked out on me."

His breath tickled her neck. "This is none of my business, but why'd you get back together with him after that?"

"Because I found out I was pregnant."

19

HE WRAPPED HIS arms around her and pulled her close to him. "What happened to the baby? Did you have another miscarriage?"

She nodded. "For a grand total of three. I may never be able to carry a baby to term."

"You could always adopt."

"Brad is against adoption," she said. "Well... I guess that's no longer my concern."

"What's wrong with adoption? The way I see it, when you enter into the partnership of marriage, you make a pact for better and for worse. If one partner is infertile, you work together to consider all your options, just as you would if you were diagnosed with cancer."

"That's easy for you to say now, Guy. But I doubt you'd feel that way if you found out you couldn't pass on your most admirable qualities to your offspring—your athletic abilities or your musical talents." Rolling onto her back, she traced his lips with her finger. "Your dazzling smile or your smoky gray eyes. It's an ego thing for men to see themselves in their children, especially their sons. It proves their manhood and validates their identity."

"That's unfair, Scottie. You're bitter now, and you have every right to be, but you can't judge every man you meet against your husband's pathetic standards."

She wanted to believe Guy was one of the good guys, like her father and Will, but she didn't know him well enough yet.

She snuggled in closer to him. "We can't fall asleep here, you know."

He moaned. "But it's so nice with the moonlight and the waves crashing."

"Do you seriously want the early-morning fitness freaks jogging past our naked bodies?"

He ran his hand across the blanket. "Our naked bodies are covered, need I remind you."

She elbowed him in the ribs. "I'm serious, Guy."

He nuzzled her neck. "We'll move in a minute."

Scottie closed her eyes. When she opened them again, the sun was full-on in the morning sky, building energy to scorch the earth with hundred-degree heat. The beach appeared deserted except for the seagulls pecking at the Doritos package by their feet and the ghost crab scuttling across the sand near Guy's head.

Scottie felt under the blanket for her clothes. She dressed quickly, sans underwear, and gently shook Guy awake.

Shielding his eyes from the sun, he looked up at her. "Morning, gorgeous." He tried to pull her to him, but she pushed him away. "I feel so gross, Guy. I'm covered in sand. Can we go somewhere to get cleaned up?"

He sat up and looked around. "No doubt a shower would be awesome right about now."

He slipped on his shorts and shook the sand off the blankets while Scottie gathered their empty cans and stuffed them in a nearby trash barrel.

"Let's get our things out of the car," Guy said. "I have an idea of where we might find a shower."

They retrieved a change of clothes, their toiletries, and the towels Scottie had purchased from Wal-Mart and traipsed back down to the beach, heading in the direction opposite the senator's rental house. "Where are we going?" she asked, struggling to keep up with him as he hurried down the beach.

"Most of these houses have outdoor showers. If we can find one that's vacant…"

"That's the most ridiculous idea I've ever heard," Scottie said. "But I'm so desperate to be clean, I'm not going to argue with you."

"There are no cars in the driveway at this house." As he started up the sandy path, over his shoulder he called, "And this one has a pool and a pool house." She followed him to the house. He checked the knob on the pool house door. "Too bad it's locked."

Scottie eyed the aqua blue water in the pool. "Why don't we get naked and jump in the pool?"

"As much as I like the idea of going skinny-dipping with you, I'd rather shower with clean water. Let's walk down the beach a little farther. If we don't find something soon, we'll come back."

They tried again at a more modest-looking home two doors down. A center bay garage with surrounding storage rooms occupied the first floor of the house. Scottie and Guy began opening and closing doors. One storage room housed a rusty grill and fishing equipment while another was packed full with boogie boards and beach chairs. Scottie peeked inside the last room. "Bingo," she said, holding the door open wide for Guy to see the fully equipped bathroom.

Guy clasped his hands together. "There is a God."

"And not a moment too soon," Scottie said, heading straight for the toilet stall.

He started the water in the shower. "We should probably shower together to save time," he said to Scottie when she finished in the toilet. "Just in case someone comes, you know."

Eager to rinse the sand off her body, she agreed. "But no funny stuff." She stripped naked, grabbed her bottles of shampoo and liquid soap, and stepped into the shower.

Guy stood in the corner of the shower, out of the way, while Scottie performed her routine. When she finished, he quickly washed and rinsed his hair and limbs. She was stepping out of the shower when he reached for her, backing her into the corner. "Not so fast."

She wrapped her arms around his neck and her legs around his waist. He took her with as much force as their slippery bodies allowed with a sense of urgency even greater than the night before. He pressed his mouth against hers to stifle her cries as she experienced wave after wave of ecstasy.

Afterwards, they clung to one another, letting the warm water massage their bodies. He lifted a wet lock of hair out of her face. "I'm pretty sure they heard you screaming all the way down on the beach."

"Good. Give them something to think about." She couldn't remember when she'd felt so naughty.

He dressed in front of the steamy mirror while she brushed her teeth and worked the tangles out of her curly hair.

"You're not seriously gonna wear that, are you?" she asked when he zipped the leather biker's vest over his bare chest.

"Hell yeah, I am." He ran his hands down the sides of the vest. "I paid fifty bucks for this beauty."

"Actually, I'm the one who wasted fifty bucks on that tacky garment. You're gonna burn up in those blue jeans, you know?" Scottie put on her black bikini, and then slipped on a pair of faded cutoff blue jeans and a white ribbed tank top.

"Sweet, a wife beater. You can be my biker chick," he said, nibbling playfully at her neck.

Scottie braided her hair into two pigtails, and then tied a pink bandanna over her head, kerchief-style.

Guy's face lit up. "A do-rag. That's what I need. Do you have another one of those?"

"Sure." Scottie tossed him a red bandanna. "But I'm gonna pretend like I don't know you if you actually wear it."

He covered his head with the bandanna and tied it at the base of his neck. "I look dope," he said, admiring his reflection in the mirror.

Scottie rolled her eyes, but secretly she thought he looked hot, leather vest and all.

*

After the previous two days, Scottie and Guy appreciated the limited travel and enjoyed the relaxed atmosphere at the events. The rally in New Bern was much like the ones in Virginia, with most of Middle Street blocked off for an old-fashioned town fair. It seemed as though everyone from Eastern North Carolina was in attendance to hear Caine's impassioned speech. Scottie and Guy worked the crowds, but no one who remotely resembled Brosnan turned up.

The senator spent the afternoon on the beaches. Clad in navy walking shorts and a plain white T-shirt, a straw hat with a red scarf tied around the band to protect her face, she hit all the popular spots—arcades and amusement parks, fishing piers and ice cream parlors.

Guy exchanged his biker costume for his bathing suit. Coated in sunscreen, barefoot and holding hands, Scottie and Guy trailed the candidate's entourage at a safe distance. Time was running out, but her mission no longer seemed as important.

She'd done the one thing she promised herself she wouldn't do. She'd fallen for Guy. And hard.

"I refuse to sleep in the car again tonight," Scottie said as they followed the Cruiser back across the causeway at the end of the day. "I don't care if I miss the perfect shot of Caine and Brosnan in a lover's embrace."

"I agree." He took a right onto West Fort Macon Road and pulled into the parking lot of a seedy-looking motel.

"This isn't exactly what I had in mind," Scottie said.

Guy killed the engine. "I hate to tell you, but this is the best we're gonna get." He opened his door to get out. "Shall I book one room or two?"

"At the risk of sounding like a slut, one." She fished her credit card out of her wallet. "Deluxe oceanfront with a king bed, please." She held the credit card out to him, but he waved it away.

"A gentleman never takes advantage of a lady on her dime."

20

TWO HOURS LATER, Scottie and Guy lay entangled in each other's arms, drowsy from their lovemaking. "I don't want to move. Let's skip tonight's event and order in a pizza," Scottie said.

"Normally I would say hell yeah, bring it on. I'd like nothing more than to spend the evening curled up with you. But I have a feeling tonight might be our night to find our man."

"You do, do you?" she asked, lifting her head off his chest. "Is this testosterone-driven intuition or is it based on information you've obtained from an insider?"

"Neither. It's a proven fact that fundraisers attract self-important men like Brosnan, much more so than free-to-anyone street carnivals like the others we've attended in the past three days."

"There you go talking like a campaign worker again."

Guy drew in a deep breath. No time like the present. He wanted his relationship with Scottie to last, more than anything he'd wanted in a long time, but he couldn't keep the truth from her any longer. "That's because I am one. I work for the GOP, Scottie. Andrew Blackmore is my boss."

Scottie stared at him, her expression impassive, without even a blink of her sexy eyelashes. And then she rolled over on her side, putting her back to him. "Are you like a campaign worker or something?"

I need to be careful here, he thought. *Less is best.* "Or something."

"Why didn't you tell me sooner?"

"Come on, Scottie. From the beginning, you've made it perfectly clear how you feel about politicians. The first night we met, at the Jefferson, you told me, and I quote, 'Most politicians I know are self-serving, backstabbing egomaniacs.' I wanted to impress you. No way was I going to confess my profession after a statement like that." He kissed the top of her head. "Please don't be mad."

"I'm not mad. I'm disappointed that you didn't trust me enough to tell me the truth sooner, regardless of my opinion about politicians." Scottie sat up in bed taking the sheet with her. "Trust is a fragile commodity, Guy. Once you lose a person's trust, it's difficult to get it back. I'm not sure I can trust you anymore. Which is problem number one."

He moaned. "What's problem number two?"

"I can't help but question your motives. Knowing you work for the Republican Party explains a lot actually," she said with a faraway look in her eyes. "Namely why you're as eager as I am to identify Brosnan. Your career depends on it. I get that. But what I want to know is, where do I fit in? I came to you for a favor, and you took advantage of my vulnerability. I presented you with a gift, a ticking time bomb that would blow the election to smithereens for the Democrats. You pounced on the opportunity, and rightly so. Any sane person would do the same in your shoes. But I can't help but think you were just using me this whole time. Which makes me question our relationship. Why did you sleep with me, Guy?"

"Because I'm crazy about you, Scottie. Because you're

beautiful and intelligent and fun as hell to be with." When he tried to stroke her arm, she brushed his hand away. "Let's be fair here. I warned you from the beginning that my involvement in your investigation was a conflict of interest. If my primary goal was to ruin the election for the Democrats, I would have leaked the photographs a long time ago. My intentions have been honorable from the beginning. And not just where you're concerned. Yes, I'd like to see the images go viral, but not until we prove Caine and Brosnan are involved. If we broke the story and it turned out Brosnan is Caine's long-lost relative, the situation could end up backfiring on the Republicans, which would hurt our campaign in the end."

Scottie relaxed a little, and settled back against the headboard. He couldn't read the expression on her face, but her body language—crossed arms and firmly set jaw—suggested she was still upset with him.

"For the record, if it makes any difference to you, I realize how wrong I was not to tell you the truth about my career from the beginning. And I'm sorry. I'm usually an up-front kind of guy."

Avoiding his gaze, she looked out of the window at the waves crashing on the shore. Five awkward minutes passed in silence. "How did you go from being a cowboy to a politician anyway?" she asked with her lips pressed tight, still staring out the window.

"Not on horseback, I can assure you of that."

She shot him an icy glare. "In case you haven't noticed, Guy, I'm not in the mood for joking."

"Sorry. I was trying to lighten the mood." He fluffed his pillow and propped it beneath his neck. "From the time I was a boy, all I ever wanted was to marry a pretty girl like my mama and run cattle for the rest of my life. Unfortunately, I have two older

Besides, those aren't the same Secret Service agents from the convention."

"If they know where you live, they know what you look like," he said.

"Maybe. Maybe not." Scottie knew she was flirting with danger, but her investigation depended on her exploring every avenue. Whether or not she unearthed any clues, Scottie had a strong feeling that making Catherine Caine's acquaintance would one day pay off. "Who knows? If I make a lasting impression, she might offer me a job as the White House press secretary when she's elected president."

"*When* she's elected president," he scoffed. "I thought our goal was to expose her affair with Brosnan so she's *not* elected president."

"Careful, Guy. You're starting to sound like a Republican." Strolling off in the direction of the candidate, she called to him over her shoulder, "Wait here. I'll be right back."

She kept an eye on the Secret Service agents while she waited her turn to speak to Catherine Caine. Both men gave her the once over, as they did everyone who approached the senator, but neither man gave her a second look.

As for the woman who stuck close to Caine, she barely glanced in her direction.

When the group ahead of her walked away, Scottie stepped up to the senator and offered her hand. "I'm Mary Scott Westport, and I'm honored to meet you. I'm impressed with your record in the Senate as well as your honest concern for the American people."

"I hope that means I can count on your support in November," Caine said.

"I'm considering it, yes. But voting for you would make me the first to vote outside of the Republican Party in my family's history." Scottie leaned into the candidate. "You won't tell my father now, will you?"

At the exact moment Catherine Caine tilted her head back and laughed, the woman standing behind Scottie—who was inappropriately dressed for her age and for the time of day—stumbled on her four-inch heels and fell into Scottie, sending Scottie's coffee down the front of Caine's blue silk sheath.

The Secret Service agents closed in around them. When Scottie saw the damage to Caine's dress, tears welled in her eyes and her hand flew to her mouth. "I'm so sorry. And embarrassed."

Alerted to the disaster, the crowd around her gasped and mumbled disapproval, making Scottie feel even worse.

The young woman with Caine rushed to her side with a handful of napkins, and began to blot the stain on the senator's dress.

"Don't worry, Mary Scott. It wasn't your fault at all. These things happen all the time." Caine lifted the silk fabric away from her body while the blotting continued. "The coffee is a little warm though."

"Thank you for being so understanding," Scottie said. "I don't imagine Andrew Blackmore would be so gracious."

Caine tilted her head back and laughed. "You're probably right. But don't tell him I said so." Then Caine turned to the young woman and said, "Thank you, Lucy. That's fine for now."

"I'd be happy to pay for your dry cleaning," Scottie offered.

"No need. I have two more dresses just like this one on the Cruiser for situations like these."

"Okay, then. I won't take up anymore of your time," Scottie said. "I'm sorry we met under these circumstances, but your kindness has earned you another fifty points in my polls."

"Well then, it was coffee well spilt," Caine said.

"I'd love to help out on your campaign. How does one go about doing that?"

"Wonderful. We are always looking for enthusiastic volunteers such as yourself." Caine motioned for her assistant. "Lucy, this is Mary Scott Westport. She's interested in working on our campaign."

Lucy keyed Scottie's name into her cell phone, then pressed a business card in her hand. "I'll have someone call you."

Scottie studied the card as she fought her way back through the crowd.

"That was some last impression you made," Guy said, shaking his head in amazement. "Only you could spill hot coffee down a senator's dress and walk away with her business card in hand."

"Don't get too excited," Scottie said, tucking the business card in her purse. "These numbers are generic, nothing I couldn't have gotten myself from the Internet."

16

MAKING GUY PROMISE not to look, Scottie climbed into the backseat on the way to Charlottesville and changed into denim shorts and a pale-blue tank. She wore the same clothes but changed her hat for the next two events, choosing first a floppy straw hat and then an Atlanta Braves baseball cap. Guy swapped out his polo shirt for a Rolling Stones tongue and lips T-shirt, a leftover from his high school days if the yellow armpits were any indication.

Much like the Sunrise Social, city executives blocked off areas of downtown for each of the remainder events on Saturday, giving the candidate an opportunity to mingle with pedestrians. Other functions were more like political rallies with local politicians speaking on behalf of the Democratic Party as well as the presidential candidate. Although her wording often varied, adapted to fit the needs of each particular town, the fundamentals of the candidate's speech were the same at every stop. She shared her position on issues like abortion and same-sex marriage, touched on her record in the Senate, expressed her concern over the recent terrorist attacks in the country, and expounded on subjects such as immigration, the state of the economy, and brothers who were first in line to inherit the family ranch. As odd man out, I had to make my own way. Good thing I got the brains in the family. Jake flunked out of college his freshman year, and Sam never bothered to apply. Both Jake and Sam got girls pregnant within six months of each other. It was almost as if they'd planned it. My father developed atrial fibrillation around that time and decided to take an early retirement. Since the ranch didn't make enough money to support three families, they cut me out completely. I was pretty pissed off at the time. Part of me still is, actually."

Scottie's face softened. "I can see why. How'd you end up on the East Coast?"

"I applied to a dozen schools, all of them as far away from my family as I could get without going abroad. I chose Carolina because they offered me the most scholarship money."

"Did you major in political science?"

"No, with law school in the back of my mind, I double-majored in English and history."

She jerked her head back. "You don't have your law degree, do you? Or have you been keeping something else from me?"

He shook his head. "My plans didn't exactly work out the way I wanted. After graduation, in order to save money for law school, I took a job writing grants for a large nonprofit in Washington. One day, the president of that nonprofit, who'd been invited to deliver the keynote address at a black-tie fundraiser, asked me to help him write his speech. Next thing I knew, I was writing speeches for half of Washington's politicians with all thoughts of going to law school forgotten."

"So you're more than just a campaign worker? You're Blackmore's speech writer?"

"Yes, I am one of several."

"You mean to tell me you're the one responsible for the bullshit the candidates preach, as you've so eloquently put it?"

He raised his right hand. "Guilty as charged. The money is good. What can I say? And the work allows me to express my feelings on a number of different topics without putting my own reputation on the line." He rolled on his side, looking up at her. "Once the election is over, when the demand for professionally written speeches declines, I will have to go back to writing grants. Unless, of course, I'm offered a job with the new administration."

"Hence the reason you want Caine's campaign to face a timely death."

21

SCOTTIE AND GUY rode in silence on the short drive to Beaufort. As hard as she tried, Scottie was having a difficult time wrapping her mind around Guy's confession. His involvement in politics wasn't the big issue. Although being confronted with the truth required an adjustment to her way of thinking about her investigation. The realization that he'd kept the truth from her, all but lied to her, made her question everything about their relationship.

She thought back to the night they first met at the Richmond airport. With his tall muscular body outfitted in a steel-gray suit, she'd deemed Guy her knight in shining armor coming to rescue the damsel in distress from a flat tire. When she learned he was returning from the Republican convention in Cleveland, she made up her mind that he worked for one of the security branches of the government, simply because a Secret Service agent was way more intriguing to her than a politician. Scottie held military men and law enforcement officers—men who place their lives on the line in order to protect their countrymen—in the highest regard. In her mind, a man who sacrifices his own needs in the service of others is the type of husband that would put his wife's and family's needs first.

When they had drinks later that night at the Jefferson, and then again in Philadelphia, she saw in him the qualities she admired—courage and compassion and humor. A man who was the polar opposite of Brad. She wanted to believe Guy was an honorable man. With her marriage falling apart, having just found her husband in bed with another woman, she needed Guy to be her paragon of virtue. And to find out he had intentionally withheld the truth from her in order to accomplish his own agenda had burst her little bubble.

Guy ran his finger down her cheek. "You look really nice tonight."

"Thanks." For the first time since they left DC, she'd had the opportunity to spend a few extra minutes on her appearance. She'd even dabbed on a little makeup and straightened her curly hair. She thought the low-cut black sundress accented her figure without revealing too much.

Although she was too angry with him to tell him so, Guy didn't look half bad himself. He'd shaven off his three-day scruff and dressed in a plaid button-down shirt and pressed khaki pants, a more casual version of the handsome man she'd met only eleven days ago. Scottie had come a long way since then, both professionally and emotionally. She'd followed Will's advice—*Be free, little birdie. Spread your wings and fly.* Professionally, she'd gone out on a limb in search of her big break. So what if she didn't hit pay dirt the first time around. There'd be other stories. The important thing was, she'd learned a lot about the integrity of journalism during her investigation.

Emotionally, after years of being trapped in an unhappy marriage, she'd allowed herself to be attracted to another man. True, she'd gotten hurt in the process, but lucky for her she'd escaped with her emotions still intact. And she wasn't eager to remarry anytime soon. She needed to stand on her own two feet before she stood with someone else. Why not enjoy her time with Guy for however long their relationship lasted? This was the last night of their road trip. Why not have wild and crazy sex with no strings attached? That's what their generation was all about anyway.

When they arrived at the waterfront in Beaufort, event planners had blocked off the boardwalk and were allowing access only to those who had purchased tickets in advance. She presented her press credentials, which entitled her to a free pass plus one, to the woman at the table. In return, she received two neon-orange wristbands.

Much like the events of the past three days, the merchants and restaurateurs along Front Street had opened their doors to the attendees, offering a large variety of seafood cooked in a number of different ways—anything from crab cakes to fried fish filets to steamed shrimp. Waiters passed samples of local craft beer, wine, and specialty drinks. Stationed at the far end of the boardwalk, out of the way of the crowd, a local band played classic country music—the likes of Patsy Cline and Randy Travis.

Scottie and Guy wandered through the crowd, taking note of the food and drink offerings before they made their choices.

"I can't believe they are charging an entrance fee for this shindig," Scottie said.

"The campaign needs to earn money at some point. They can't afford to give everything away. In the grand scheme of things, fifty bucks isn't that much. I've been to political dinners that brought thousands of dollars a plate." He took her by the elbow and led her to the edge of the dock beside the boats. He bent down to kiss her and she let him. "I'm glad you got us in for free, but I would've been happy to pay for both our tickets. You're not a cheap date, Scottie. Don't ever let anyone treat you like you are one. Capeesh?"

"Capeesh," she said and kissed him back with more fervor

than before. "Now, let's get a drink." She dragged him through the crowd to the nearest bar.

"What're you in the mood for?" he asked.

"Hmm, something refreshing." Tapping her chin, she stared up at the sky while the bartender waited patiently for her order. "How about a Moscow Mule?"

"Good choice. Make that two of them," Guy said to the bartender.

Drinks in hand, they filled cocktail-size plates with samples of dishes, then located an empty table. They found the evening breeze refreshing after the heat of the day, and for the first time in as long as Scottie could remember, she felt content.

"I could sit here all night and watch the boats tie up at the marina, but I guess we better get to work." She tossed the last shrimp in her mouth and washed it down with the remainder of her Moscow Mule.

A half hour later, Scottie was shooting candids of the crowd when Guy's cell phone vibrated. He checked the caller ID. "I need to take this." He held his finger up to her, indicating he'd only be a minute, and crossed the boardwalk for privacy.

She snapped a few shots of Guy talking on the phone to remember him by when he returned to Washington and she went home to Richmond. She was scanning the faces of the crowd with her camera when her mystery man came into focus on her viewfinder. He was dressed as though he'd stepped off a yacht in a blue blazer and white linen slacks. She held her finger on the shutter, allowing the camera to tick off twenty continuous shots of Brosnan as he walked into the bar where they'd gotten their Moscow Mules.

She considered her options. She didn't need any more photographs of Brosnan locking lips with the senator. All she needed was a name. Shoving her camera in her bag, she pulled a floppy sunhat over her blonde hair, and followed him inside.

"Is this seat taken?" she asked Brosnan, her hand on the back of the empty bar stool next to him.

His eyes roamed her body in a way that made her feel dirty. "Not for you, pretty lady."

"I'm Mary Scott Westport." She held her hand out to him. "And you are?"

His hand was cold and dry. "Delighted to meet you."

Fine by me if he wants to play hard to get, she thought. *Because I have no intention of giving up easily.*

The bartender set what appeared to be a Scotch on the rocks in front of Brosnan. "Anything for you?" Brosnan asked Scottie.

"Thanks, but I'm fine." Once the bartender was out of earshot, she asked, "Have you met the candidate yet? I think Senator Caine is quite impressive."

"She's no different than any other politician I've ever met. They can all be had for a price."

At a total loss of how to respond, Scottie decided to play the roll of dumb blonde. "I like the sound of that." She walked her fingers up his coat sleeve. "You must be a rich and powerful man. What line of work are you in?"

"Import, export." He glanced around the room. "It's crowded in here. Shall we go to my hotel room where we can talk in private?"

Scottie had no intention of going anywhere with this slick-talking sleazeball, even if it cost her her big break. "I don't think my boyfriend would like that very much."

"What a pity. I was prepared to offer you an evening of intense pleasure." Brosnan waved at someone behind Scottie. "I best be on my way, then. My associate is waiting for me." He slapped a ten-dollar bill on the bar and left the restaurant.

*

Scottie waited thirty seconds, then slid off her bar stool and trailed Brosnan at a safe distance through the throng of people on Front Street. She texted Guy as she walked: *In hot pursuit of Brosnan.* She stuffed the phone back into her bag. She couldn't let her mystery man get away this time. She needed to find a way to identify him, and a license plate number would work just fine.

She dropped back twenty feet when he left the waterfront area and headed down a side street. Keeping a safe distance, she followed him down the street a block, then into a parking lot and through several rows of cars. When he stopped and looked around as though he sensed someone watching him, she ducked behind a nearby car and waited until he moved on. She lost sight of him altogether and raced through the maze of cars in a panicked search. She was ready to give up and head back to the waterfront when a beast of a man jumped out of a dark-gray SUV and grabbed her, knocking her sunhat off and sending her handbag crashing to the ground. He wrapped a muscular arm around her waist and clamped a beefy hand over her mouth.

Scottie had taken a self-defense class at UVA. "Claw his eyes out," her instructor had lectured over and over until it was ingrained in her memory. "Kick him where it counts. Fight dirty if you have to, but fight. Once he gets you in his car, your chances of surviving decrease dramatically."

Her screams were muffled by the beast's massive hand. Squirming as best she could, she kicked at his shins and threw elbows to his ribs. He lifted her off the ground with ease and held her there, her feet dangling in the air. "Stop fighting or I'll break your neck," a deep voice with a hint of a foreign accent whispered in her ear.

Scottie grew still and he lowered her back down to the

ground. Brosnan appeared from around the front of the SUV. "Well, what do we have here? If it isn't the amateur sleuth Scottie Darden in person," he said, his expression smug.

Scottie's eyes grew wide. He'd set her up.

"That's right, Ms. Darden. All this time you've been looking for me, I've been following you." He held his hand out to her. "Give me the memory card from your camera? I want to destroy the shots you took of me tonight."

The beast loosened his grip enough for Scottie to grab her bag off the ground and remove her camera. She released the memory card and handed it to Brosnan. The photos she'd taken of Brosnan on the waterfront were of no use to her anyway.

He slipped the card into the inside pocket of his linen sport coat. "My friend here is going to remove his hand from your mouth so we can talk, but if you try to scream he will slice your pretty face into a million pieces with this." The beast let go of her mouth, produced a switchblade from somewhere, most likely his pocket, and held it inches from her face.

"Who are you?" Scottie demanded.

"You don't get to ask the questions, Ms. Darden. In case you haven't noticed, you are not in control of the situation." He took a step closer to her. "Let's talk about the other files. We found the thumb drive in your box of tampons—a clever deterrent for most men but we are not dissuaded by feminine hygiene."

Her confusion turned to fear when she realized these men had gotten close enough to her to go through all of her belongings without her knowing it. If they found the drive in her tampon box, they'd undoubtedly located the files on her computer and iPad as well. She'd been too busy making love to Guy and too distracted by the revelation that he worked for the Republican Party to realize the photographs were missing. "How? When?"

Scottie asked, but Brosnan shut her up with a menacing glare that made her blood run cold.

"I warned you, Ms. Darden, about asking questions. However, lucky for you, this is one I'm happy to answer." He chuckled, a strangled sound that resonated pure evil. "I'll start with when. Last night while you were making love with your boyfriend under the moonlight. A bit cliché for my tastes but sweet nonetheless." He fingered a lock of Scottie's hair. "You really shouldn't leave your car doors unlocked. You never know who might be in the area." He twisted the lock of hair around his finger, and then grabbed a whole handful, yanking Scottie's head toward him. "We erased the image files from the drives on your computer and iPad, both hard and cloud. I'm only going to ask you this question once. If you lie to me, and those images go public, we'll hunt you down and my associate will end your life in a most unpleasant way. Do we understand one another?"

Scottie nodded her head vigorously.

"Are there any other copies of the files?"

Since they hadn't mentioned the memory card—the original one with the raw images hidden in the lining of her electronics bag—she prayed that meant they hadn't found it.

She shook her head no. "You found them all."

"Good." He let go of her hair. "I would hate to have to kill someone so young and pretty, but I can promise you—"

"Let her go." Guy stepped out from behind the SUV with his cell phone pressed to his ear. "I'm on the phone with the FBI. In less than three minutes, one of their SWAT teams will descend upon this parking lot—just like the American troops who landed at Normandy on D-Day. I know who you are, Mikhail Popkov, Russian mob king and sex slave trader." Guy held his phone out. "More importantly, the FBI knows who you are."

22

WHEN THE BEAST loosened his grip on Scottie, she elbowed him in the face, breaking his nose on impact. With blood gushing from his nose, he dropped the switchblade and called out in pain.

"Run, Scottie," Guy shouted, and they took off across the parking lot. Thankful she'd worn her flat sandals instead of heels, she ran as fast as she could until she reached the edge of the crowd at the waterfront.

When Scottie and Guy heard the squealing wheels of the SUV peeling out of the parking lot, they slowed down long enough to catch their breath, and then took off running again down a side street to Robbie's Jeep.

Once they were safely inside the car, struggling to catch his breath, Guy asked, "Where'd you learn to fight like that?"

"I took self-defense in college. I had an overly eager professor."

"You broke that man's nose. And he was no ordinary-size man. That dude was a giant, close to seven feet if I had to guess." Guy offered up a high five. "Remind me never to make you mad again."

"He's a beast all right. I hope I never run into him in a dark alley." She mopped sweat from her brow with a pink bandanna. "You know, now that I think about it, he might be the limo driver, the one who was driving Brosnan the night of the convention." She paused. "I guess we can call him by his real name. What'd you say it was, Pop something?"

"Popkov. It's Russian," he said. "And that would make sense that he was driving him the night of the convention. More than likely he's Popkov's bodyguard doing double duty as his limo driver."

Guy's cell phone rang. He listened for a few seconds before he reported, "They're headed west on Highway 70, driving a charcoal-gray late-model Cadillac Escalade with Pennsylvania plates. I didn't get the number."

"The FBI I presume?" Scottie asked when he ended the call.

"Yes. The local branch. Let's hope they catch them."

"I'm gonna be looking over my shoulder for the rest of my life if they don't." Scottie settled back in the seat. "Start talking. Tell me everything you know and how you know it."

Guy started the car and pulled away from the curb. "I got a call from Rich, who finally caught up with his contact at the FBI. Baird recognized our man right away. Apparently they've been after Mikhail Popkov for some time. He is a Russian mob boss who lives in the United States illegally and is wanted for a long list of crimes."

"How did you make contact with the local FBI?"

"I was on the phone with Baird when your text came through. When I told him you'd spotted Popkov, he patched me through to the local authorities."

A fleet of vehicles flashing blue lights passed them headed in the opposite direction. "And there they go." The reality of what just happened settled over Scottie. "They broke into our car last night and erased the images from my computer and iPad." She shivered. "It makes my skin crawl to think of them watching us having sex on the beach."

"They couldn't have seen much."

"On a full moon, I'm sure they saw plenty."

"Try not to think about it, Scottie. Popkov and his sidekick were more interested in getting their hands on the digital files than watching us. I hope you have another copy."

"Unfortunately, they found that one too." A feeling deep inside her gut—no doubt brought on by the recent discovery that he worked for the Republican Party—warned her not to tell him about the memory card hidden in her electronics bag.

When they arrived back at the hotel, Guy entered the room first, inspecting the bathroom and under the bed and behind the curtains for unwanted guests. He bolted the door behind them and went out on the balcony to make another call. Scottie watched him through the sliding glass doors as he paced back and forth with one hand clutching his cell phone to his ear and the other raking through his cropped hair.

She crawled into bed fully clothed and pulled the covers up over her head. She'd made a colossal mess of her investigation. All the time she'd been in search of Popkov like a hunter tracking his prey, he'd been watching her like a preschool teacher minding her students on the playground. She'd nearly gotten herself killed tonight. What had she been thinking following a strange man into a dark empty parking lot? And what about Guy? If anything had happened to him, she would never be able to forgive herself for dragging him into her investigation. And how did Catherine Caine play into any of it? *She's no different from any other politician I've ever met. They can all be had for a price.* What exactly had Popkov meant by that statement? He certainly didn't sound like a man talking fondly about his lover. Was he bribing her for some reason?

Scottie turned out the lights and pretended to be asleep when Guy came back inside. Peeping through one eye, she watched him feel his way through the darkened room to the bathroom. She heard the toilet flush, then the water running in the sink. When he came out of the bathroom, he crawled in bed beside her. She heard his thumbs tapping on the screen of his phone as he typed out a text, followed by the unmistakable vibration of a response coming in.

Who was he so busy texting? And why the need for secrecy? Who had he been talking to out on the balcony? What had they said that they didn't want her to hear?

She fell asleep waiting for the texting to end, and woke again around five thirty the following morning. Guy was snoring softly beside her. She tiptoed around the room, locating Guy's cell phone on the bedside table and picking up her electronics bag from the chair in the corner where she'd dropped it the night before.

She went in the bathroom and locked the door. She pressed the home button on Guy's cell and the screen lit up. When she unlocked the phone, she was surprised to find it wasn't password protected. She glanced at the closed door. "Tsk, tsk. You shouldn't be so trusting, Guy," she mumbled. She opened his message app and clicked on the thread from Rich, her heart racing as she scrolled through their conversation from the night before.

Rich: *This whole thing might blow up in our faces if we don't post the pictures soon.*

Guy: *Does Baird know about the senator?*

Rich: *Not yet but he's asking a lot of questions. I can't hold him off much longer.*

Guy: *What about Blackmore?*

Rich: *James is briefing him as we speak.*

Guy: *Popkov deleted the files. She doesn't have any copies.*

Rich: *The FBI can retrieve them from her hard drive.*

Guy: *Scottie will never let them have access to her computer.*

Rich: *The FBI will confiscate it.*

Guy: *Not without a search warrant.*

Rich: *Don't try to play hardball with the FBI. You won't win.*

Guy: *I'm not calling the shots.*

Rich: *Clearly. I told you not to let her out of your sight, and she started a gang war with a Russian mob boss. Great job, Jordan.*

Scottie slid down the wall to the tile floor. *I told you not to let her out of your sight.* What was that supposed to mean? Had Guy merely been following orders when he agreed to come on this road trip with her? Was the sex simply a bonus for a job well done?

Scottie's pulse quickened and she broke out in a sweat. She thumbed a text to Rich: *Nobody takes advantage of me and gets away with it. XOXO Scottie.*

She spread a towel out and dumped the contents of her electronics bag onto the bathroom floor. Amongst the lens and other camera accessories, she spotted Senator Caine's business card. She picked it up, scanning through the various numbers for the Democratic Party and Caine's campaign headquarters. *I'll have to try a more direct route.* She grabbed a pen from the pile on the towel and jotted a quick note on the back, then set the card on the bathroom floor beside her.

She found the slit she'd made in the lining of the bag and ripped it open wide enough to fit her hand through. She shook the bag around until she located the memory card. This time she only uploaded the images to her iPad, not her computer. She placed the memory card inside the case of her cell phone—the one item she rarely let out of her sight.

Scottie got to her feet and returned her equipment to her electronics bag. She brushed her teeth and hair and wiped the smeared mascara from beneath her eyes. She found the keys to Robbie's Jeep in the pocket of Guy's shorts, which he'd discarded on the floor beside the toilet. The sun was rising over the ocean, filling their room with pink light, when she opened the bathroom door. Guy's phone vibrated in her hand with an incoming call from Rich. She answered it.

"Good morning, Rich. Scottie Darden here. Let me get Guy on the phone for you. He's right here in bed beside me. He deserves a raise by the way. He's done such a commendable job of not letting me out of his sight."

23

SCOTTIE HAD BACKED out of the parking space and was switching gears from reverse to drive when Guy appeared in front of her in his boxer shorts. "Wait, Scottie! Where are you going?" He pounded on the hood of the Jeep.

She rolled down her window. "To meet with Catherine Caine. Now get out of my way."

He crossed his arms and planted his feet firmly on the ground. "Not until you tell me what's going on."

She blasted the horn, but when he refused to move, she yelled, "I'll give you exactly one minute."

He walked around to the driver's side window. "Why are you so upset? I don't understand what you said to Rich on the phone."

"You're a good detective. Figure it out for yourself. I gotta go. I'm going to be late for my meeting."

"I'm going with you. Baird wants to see both of us right away." Guy looked down at his seminaked body. "It'll just take a minute for me to put on some clothes."

When she started to drive off, he ran along side of the Jeep. "Wait, stop! Why are you leaving me?"

She slammed her foot on the brake. "I read your texts, Guy.

It's okay for you to let me out of your sight now. Your presence is no longer needed in my investigation."

He looked at the phone in his hand, then stared back at Scottie dumbfounded. "You read my texts?"

"Damn straight I did. You should consider password protection from now on."

He hung his head. "God, Scottie, I can only imagine what you must be thinking, but you've got it all wrong."

"You have no idea what I'm thinking," she said, and peeled out of the parking lot, leaving him staring at her taillights.

*

"I need to see Senator Caine right away," Scottie said to the two Secret Servicemen stationed outside the front door of the beach house.

The heavier of the two agents gave Scottie the once over. "Do you have an appointment?"

"No, but I promise you it's a matter of urgency."

"I'm sorry," the other agent said. His eyes were kind despite his tight lips. "We can't let you in unless you have an appointment."

"Will you at least give her this?" Scottie handed the agent Caine's business card. On the back, she'd written in tiny print: *I need to speak with you right away about the photographs I took in the alley behind the convention center in Philadelphia.*

The nice agent took the card from Scottie and went inside. Caine's assistant, Lucy, appeared less than a minute later.

"I remember you," she said. "You're the one who spilt coffee on the senator in Leesburg."

Scottie held out her hand. "I'm Scottie Darden."

"I understand you're requesting to see the senator. Can you tell me what this urgent matter is about?" Lucy asked.

Scottie removed her iPad from her bag and held it out so Lucy could see the photographs.

Lucy stiffened. She gestured at the Secret Servicemen. "These men will need to check your bag."

The agents surrounded Scottie, one of them rummaging through her bag while the other quickly patted her down.

"Come with me, please," Lucy said when the agents finished their search. She whisked Scottie through a living room packed with people, mostly men, and down a short hall. "Wait here." She pointed to a wooden chair beside a closed door. Lucy tapped on the door and disappeared inside. She emerged two minutes later. "The senator will see you now."

Lucy ushered Scottie into the dining room, which was serving as the senator's makeshift office.

Senator Caine stood to greet her. "It's nice to see you again, Mary Scott, or should I call you Scottie?" If Caine was annoyed at Scottie for intentionally trying to mislead her by using a different name when they'd met in Leesburg, she didn't show it.

"Please call me Scottie. My mother is the only person who calls me Mary Scott, and only when she's angry."

The senator smiled. "Please, have a seat."

Scottie took the seat opposite her. "Thank you for seeing me on such short notice. I promise I won't take too much of your time." She placed her iPad on the table in front of the senator and scrolled through each of the three images. "Please believe me, senator. I never meant you any harm when I took these. All I wanted was a behind-the-scenes photograph of you with your family."

"I wondered what happened to these. Why haven't you released them to the media?" Caine scrolled through the images again. "Although I must say I'm glad you didn't. I can see how they might be misinterpreted."

"My conscience wouldn't let me post the story until I verified the facts. I haven't been able to identify the man in the photographs until last night."

Caine's eyebrows shot up. "You mean Logan James?"

Scottie hesitated. "I don't know who Logan James is, but this man"—she pointed to the photograph—"is a Russian mobster named Mikhail Popkov."

"I don't understand," the senator said.

"There's a lot I don't understand as well." Scottie sat back in her chair.

"The FBI is here waiting to brief me on the case. If you don't object, I'll invite them to join us. Hopefully they can shed some light on the situation."

Scottie nodded her consent. The senator texted her assistant, asking her to show the men in.

Scottie was surprised to see a disheveled Guy amongst the throng of dark suits that crowded into the dining room. She was even more blown away when the senator greeted Guy and the smug-looking young man who walked in behind Guy by name. "If it isn't Rich Cartwright and Guy Jordan. It's not every day I have the pleasure of meeting with top GOP brass."

Top GOP brass. WTF.

Guy was quick to grab the empty seat next to Scottie. "We need to talk," he whispered in her ear as he lowered himself to the chair.

"Fine, you can start by telling me what Rich is doing here."

"Your guess is as good as mine," Guy said. "I assume Baird dragged him along."

Rich sat down next to Baird on the other side of the table from Scottie and Guy. She glared at Rich and he smirked at her in return. She immediately disliked him. She'd known too many Riches in her lifetime, boys from privileged families who felt entitled to whatever they wanted. They cheated on tests. Took advantage of girls who drank too much. Butted their noses into investigations that didn't concern them.

Senator Caine spread her hands flat on the table. "Now that you have my attention, Mr. Baird, to what do I owe this honor?"

Scottie guessed Roger Baird to be in his midthirties. His piercing blue eyes and deep voice commanded authority. "We have a situation, Senator, regarding certain photographs that were taken by Ms. Darden—"

The senator cut him off. "I've seen the images."

Guy turned to Scottie. "But... I thought..."

Scottie shrugged and looked away from him.

Baird coughed into his hand. "We were under the impression Ms. Darden was no longer in possession of the digital files." His eyes met Scottie's. "May I see them?"

"That's up to the senator," Scottie said.

All eyes zeroed in on Caine, who nodded her approval.

Scottie slid her iPad across the table to Baird, and with Rich peering over his shoulder, he scrolled through the files. "The senator is cropped out of the images I've seen." He turned to Caine. "Are you aware that the man in the photograph, a Russian mob boss named Mikhail Popkov, is on the FBI's most wanted list?"

"No, I was not aware of that," Caine said. "I'd never met the man until that night. I was told he was a Texas oil millionaire named Logan James."

"I mean no disrespect, Senator," Baird said. "But this exchange between you and Popkov is awfully familiar for two people who've never met."

"I agree wholeheartedly, Mr. Baird." The senator's lips tightened, but she managed to maintain her composure. "I've met all kinds of people during my career as a politician. I stopped being surprised by the things my constituents say and do a long time ago."

"Who arranged the meeting for you?" Baird asked.

"One of my most loyal supporters. I'm happy to provide his contact information if you'd like to speak with him. This supporter told me he had a friend with a lot of money who was interested in making a contribution to my campaign as well as a sizable donation to the Democratic Party. I take fundraising very seriously, Mr. Baird. Obviously. I'm running for president of the United States."

"And did your staff vet this man, this Logan James?" Baird asked.

"Yes. Neither our background check nor the referrals he provided presented any red flags."

Scottie detected a hint of sarcasm in his voice when Baird asked, "Whose idea was it to meet in a dark alley?"

"I've met supporters in much stranger places than a dark alley, Mr. Baird," Caine said, managing to keep a straight face. "The arrangement was mutually agreed upon by my assistant and Mr. James. He had an early flight out of Philadelphia the next morning to Dallas. The only time available in my schedule was those few brief moments after the convention before I needed to leave for the reception."

Baird turned his attention to Scottie. "Is this the only copy you have left of the images?"

Scottie thought about the memory card concealed inside her phone case. "Yes." She didn't trust the card in the hands of the FBI. She would destroy it herself when she got home.

"You realize the photographs would do considerable damage to my campaign," Caine said to Scottie.

"Which is why I plan to delete them," Scottie said. "Not to

mention the fact that Popkov threatened to kill me if I released them. As far as I'm concerned this investigation is closed."

"In that case, let me delete them for you." Rich snatched the iPad from Baird. "You have to take an additional step in order to permanently delete images from an Apple mobile device." His fingers traveled across the screen too fast for Scottie to see what he was doing with the images.

Scottie held out her hand. "Give me back my iPad, Rich. I'm a photojournalist. I know how to manage digital files."

He handed her back the device. "I was just trying to help."

Baird opened a laptop and turned it around so the group could see the image on the screen. "We've been working this case for years, and thanks to Scottie's photographs, we have our first major break."

Scottie squinted her eyes at the passport photograph of Popkov.

"The name on this passport is Logan James. Is this the same man who confronted you in the parking lot last night?" Baird asked Scottie, and she nodded.

Baird scrolled through several more images of US passports. "Notice that his name is different on every passport." Popkov had facial hair in some. In others he was clean-shaven. He had long hair, short hair, dark hair, and gray hair. But the blue eyes were every bit as cold in all of them.

"Seven different passports, seven different names, from seven different states," Baird said. "Texas, Wyoming, Nevada, Washington, California, Florida, and Arizona." He clicked on an image of a Russian passport. "This is the real man—Russian born and bred, Mikhail Popkov. He's worth several billion dollars. And he's wanted on drug and sex trafficking charges, and for questioning in several murder cases. And that doesn't even include the extortion allegations."

"Which is where I come into play," Caine said. "He makes large contributions to political campaigns in exchange for unethical favors."

"Bingo," Baird said. "Did Popkov aka Logan James make any specific requests when you met him in the alley?"

Caine smiled at Scottie. "We hardly had time to talk before our resident paparazzo scared him away."

Baird appeared satisfied with her answer. "We checked with your assistant. As of a few minutes ago, your campaign has not received a contribution from anyone using any of the names on these passports." He gestured at his computer. "According to your assistant, Logan James has made no further contact with your office. Has he reached out to you directly?"

"Most definitely not, Mr. Baird," Caine said in an irritated tone.

"Needless to say, we have concerns for your safety, Senator," Baird said. "We have taken measures to beef up your security."

Caine peered at Baird over the top of her reading glasses. "I'm not worried about my safety, Mr. Baird. I'm surrounded by my Secret Service agents 24/7. But I am worried about Scottie. Are you offering her protection?"

"We can certainly do that," Baird said.

"Good! Then I guess that means we're done here." Caine rose from the table, and everyone stood to leave. She pulled Scottie aside. "If I'm elected in November, I want you to call me. I will be looking for staff members with your honesty and integrity. You're a breath of fresh hair in a complicated world full of corruption and hate."

24

AFTER THE MEETING adjourned, Scottie bolted for the front door with Guy hot on her heels.

"Wait, Scottie. You can't just leave me here."

"Why don't you catch a ride with your best friend, Rich?" she yelled over her shoulder.

"But I promised Robbie I'd bring him back his car."

"Fine, take it." She tossed the car keys to him over her head.

She wove her way through the maze of cars parked haphazardly in the driveway. When she got to the street, she took off running, ignoring the dark clouds brewing in the west. Her legs ached with pent-up energy. She needed to cut loose and fly, to release the anger and hurt and humiliation.

She was half a mile down the road when Guy pulled up alongside her. "Look, Scottie. I know you're mad at me, but at least give me a chance to explain."

She slowed to a walk. "What's left to explain? You're a key player in the Republican Party. I get it. You were just doing your job, and the sex was your bonus."

"You know that's not true." He leaned across the seat and opened the passenger door. "Get in the car. It's a long way back to the motel, and there's a storm system moving in."

She stopped walking and pondered the darkening cloud behind her. "Fine, but only because I don't want to get struck by lightning." She got in the car. "I have nothing to say to you."

"Then I'll talk and you listen." He started driving in the direction of the hotel. "But I don't really know where to start."

"Exactly. You've dug your grave so deep, nothing you can say will help you climb out."

He glanced over at her. "Regardless of what Rich wanted, I'm the one who made the decision to go on this road trip with you. I never tried to hide my feelings for you."

"Right, you tried to pick me up the first time we met at the Richmond airport, even though you knew I was married."

He pounded the steering wheel. "You're twisting everything around."

"No, Guy, that's your job. Twisting things around is what politicians do."

He threw his hands up. "I admit it. I should have told you about my job from the start."

"Well, duh!" She bared her teeth. "You're such a liar. Even when you confessed to being a politician, you left out the most important part. You're not just working on the campaign. You're considered top brass in the Republican Party."

His shoulders slumped. "Either way, my involvement in your investigation was a conflict of interest. I tried to tell you that, if you remember correctly."

"An honest man would have tried harder. But you couldn't walk away from the chance to bring the election to a screeching halt for the Democrats. Tell me, Guy, does being the Republican Party Hero come with a big fat promotion and raise?"

His face tightened. "You begged me, Scottie. You told me you had no one else to turn to. Someone had already ransacked your house. I wasn't about to let you go off and get yourself killed, which would've happened last night if I hadn't been there. Yes, I should've come clean with you from the start. But I didn't, and I'm sorry for that." He drove into the motel parking lot and turned off the car. He shifted in his seat to face her. "The truth is, my feelings for you clouded my vision. The more time we spent together, the harder I fell for you. I haven't felt like this about anyone in a long time. If ever. I had dug myself into a deep hole. I was terrified you would bury me when you found out the truth."

"I'm not going to bury you, Guy. I just don't want anything else to do with you." She got out of the car, and as the first drops of rain began to fall, she dashed up the stairs to their room. She was gathering her belongings in her suitcase by the time Guy walked in.

"What're you doing?" he asked.

"What does it look like I'm doing? I'm packing. I'm going to rent a car and drive home." She went to the bathroom for her toiletries.

"That's ridiculous," Guy said, following her into the bathroom. "I'm driving right through Richmond. I can easily drop you off."

"No thanks," she said, zipping up her cosmetic case.

She tried to push him out of her way, but he took her by the arms. "You shouldn't be alone right now, Scottie. The FBI has offered you protection. If you won't let me help you, at least let them."

She stared him down. "Because they didn't do their job and Popkov is still on the loose?" She wrangled free of him. "I don't need their protection. I'm leaving for Rio in two days, and there's a good chance I won't be coming back."

She hadn't thought about it until that very moment, but the idea of disappearing to someplace remote and tropical felt liberating. *Be free, little birdie. Go forth and fly.*

"What would you do then, become a beach bum?" Guy said. "You won't be able to post any photographs, at least not under your byline."

"I'm done with investigative journalism." She tossed her cosmetic case in her suitcase and wheeled it to the door. "Maybe I'll change my name and become a nature photographer. But whatever I decide to do, it won't be for you to worry about."

*

Scottie drove six hours through pouring rain as she headed north from Morehead City to Reagan National Airport in Washington. She returned her rental car, and then took the Metro to Guy's apartment building in Logan circle where she retrieved her Mini and got back on the interstate, this time heading south to Richmond. With two restroom breaks, one trip through the drive-through at Chick-fil-A in Roanoke Rapids, work zone backups near Alexandria, and rush hour traffic north of Richmond, she arrived home just before six o'clock on Tuesday evening.

She was none-too-pleased to find an unmarked car parked in front of her house.

Two FBI agents greeted her on the sidewalk as she wheeled her suitcase to the front door. "Evening, ma'am. We're with the FBI." The taller of the two stepped forward. "I'm Agent Kennedy and this is my partner Nixon." They simultaneously flashed their badges at her.

"Wait. Kennedy and Nixon. That's a bit of a coincidence. You didn't actually guard those presidents, did you?"

Nixon, who kind of looked like Richard Nixon with a nose that spread across his face and dark hair balding at both temples, was quick to say, "No, ma'am. We're not that old,"

Scottie did the mental math. "Oh, right, my bad. That would make you at least eighty."

"We have orders to protect you, ma'am," Kennedy said.

"Thanks anyway, but I don't need protection," Scottie said, searching her bag for her house keys.

"We can't ignore orders, ma'am," Kennedy said. "We need to search the premises before you enter the house."

A vision of Mikhail Popkov lying in wait for her, hiding in her downstairs powder room, popped into her head. "I guess there's no harm in that. I'll warn you, though. I haven't had a chance to straighten up since the last time these Russian mobsters ransacked my house." She pushed the door open, then took a step back allowing them entry ahead of her.

Weapons drawn, Kennedy and Nixon made their way to the back of the house. Closing the door behind her, Scottie parked her suitcase at the bottom of the stairs and entered her immaculate living room. *Will.*

She texted her brother: *I owe you one.*

He responded right away: *Actually you owe my cleaning service two hundred dollars. Consider it an early Christmas present. Are you home from your adventure?*

Scottie: *Yep. Just walked in.*

Will: *Cool. I'll stop by on my way home.*

Scottie: *That's not a good idea. I don't want you tangled up in this mess I created for myself.*

Will: *I'm on my way.*

Scottie: *Seriously. I'm fine. The FBI is here to protect me.*

Will: *Leaving the office now.*

Room by room, Kennedy and Nixon checked every inch of her house for intruders. They even had handheld gadgets to check for listening devices. Once they declared the house safe,

Kennedy said, "We'll be in the car out front if you need anything."

Scottie walked them to the front door. "I don't mean to be ungrateful, but I'm really fine here by myself. My brother is on his way over. If it makes you feel better, I can get him to stay here with me. At least for the next two days, until I leave for the Olympics in Rio."

The agents exchanged a look Scottie couldn't interpret. "What time is your flight on Thursday?" Kennedy asked. "We'll plan your transfer to the airport, to make sure you're not followed."

As much as she hated to admit it, Scottie liked the idea of having a private escort to the airport. She certainly didn't want to drag Popkov and company to Rio with her. "Around six p.m., I think. But I'll have to check and let you know."

Kennedy jotted the information down on a small notepad he kept in his inside suit pocket. "If you will confirm your itinerary, we will have someone make the arrangements. Also, Baird has scheduled a meeting with our sketch artist for two o'clock tomorrow afternoon. He asked that you work with her by telling her whatever you remember about Popkov's assistant."

"I didn't see that much of his face," Scottie said. "He was behind me most of the time, but I'll tell her what I remember."

"In the meantime, we'll have a team guarding your house around the clock," Nixon said. "We change shifts every eight hours—at seven, three, and eleven."

She cast a nervous glance at the house across the street, where her elderly neighbor kept tabs on Scottie through her upstairs bedroom window. "I'm sure my neighbors will love that."

"Ma'am," Nixon said, his tone solemn. "I think you're underestimating the seriousness of the situation. Mikhail Popkov is wanted on murder and sex trafficking charges, and a whole host of drug-related felonies. We are not dealing with nice people." He handed her a business card with one number printed on it. "The team stationed in front of your house will be in possession of this cell phone at all times. If anything arises your suspicion, you call this number." He jabbed at the card with his long finger. "Even if you hear a scratching sound in your attic that turns out to be a mouse, it's our job to check it out."

"I don't have mice in my attic, Agent Nixon, but I hear you loud and clear. You've succeeded in scaring the shit out of me. I'm pretty sure I won't sleep for the rest of my life."

"Oh, you'll sleep alright. Just not until this evil bastard is behind bars."

25

WILL ARRIVED AT her door ten minutes later with a twelve-pack of Blue Moon beer, a bottle of chilled Chardonnay, and his phone glued to his ear.

"Who are you talking to?" She relieved him of his burden, and walked the beer and wine back to the kitchen.

"I'm on hold with Chanello's," he said, following her. "I'm starving. Do you want pepperoni or sausage?"

"Both." Scottie opened a beer and handed it to Will. "For a moment there, I thought you were calling Mom and Dad."

He dropped to a bar stool. "I did that on the way over here. Lucky for you they're boarding a plane for Anchorage. Otherwise they'd be sharing your bed tonight."

Scottie smacked her forehead. "I forgot about their anniversary cruise. I meant to order flowers for their stateroom."

Will held the phone away from his mouth. "We still have time to do that tomorrow."

Scottie filled a wine glass to the rim with Chardonnay. "What did you tell them?"

"Only what I know, that you'd gotten in over your head in one of your investigations. I assured them they had no reason to worry since the FBI is acting as your personal bodyguards."

"I'm sure they're freaking out."

"Of course," Will said. "As you might imagine, Dad was spouting lists of names of people who might be able to help and Mom was praying."

"So much for their Happy Bon Voyage. Poor Mom and Dad can't even celebrate their thirty-fifth wedding anniversary without worrying about their troubled child." Will shot her a look and she added, "Sorry. Let me be sure to make the distinction. Their troubled *daughter*, I mean."

When the pizza person came on the line, Will recited their order, waited for the amount, and hung up.

"Wonder if my bodyguards will let the delivery man come to the door," Scottie said.

"Depends on which delivery guy it is. If it's the one I'm thinking of, he might enjoy being frisked."

"I'm going to pretend you didn't say that." She left him sitting by himself at the kitchen counter and walked to the windows in the adjoining room, staring through the plantation shutters to the courtyard.

Will got up and followed her into the other room. "So…" He dropped down in the leather chair, and kicked his feet up on the ottoman. "I assume this current drama has to do with the photographs you took of Senator Caine. Tell me everything, and don't leave out the part about the sex and heartbreak."

Scottie jerked her head back, away from the window and toward him. "How'd you know?"

"Seriously? Your cheeks are all rosy, and the spark has returned to your eyes. You've been walking around here like a zombie for as long as I can remember. Whoever he is, he made you feel something again, although I'm getting a vibe that that something might not be bliss."

She sighed. "I can't get anything past you."

"Nope. You never have been able to hide your feelings from me."

"I have this creepy feeling someone is watching us." She closed all the shutters in the room, and then sank down to the sofa opposite him "I've really done it this time, bro. As if my life wasn't already messed up enough with my screwed-up marriage. I started a gang war with a Russian Mob boss."

Will sat up straighter in his chair. "I think you need to begin at the beginning."

She told him the whole story, from meeting Guy in the airport to her close encounter with Popkov in Beaufort the night before. "It's all your fault, Will. You told this little birdie to go forth and fly, and look where it got me."

"Pu-lease, Scottie. I didn't mean for you to take on the Russian mob."

The doorbell rang, and she went to answer it with Will on her heels.

She thought she knew them all by heart, but Scottie had never seen this particular delivery person. Small in stature, he looked like he was fifteen, more a boy than a man, probably a VCU college student going through late puberty.

"Dude." The delivery boy pointed at the unmarked sedan at the curb. "That guy in that car right there asked to see my ID. Am I in some kind of trouble?"

Will brushed Scottie aside and reached for his wallet. "You're fine. It's my sister they are here for. She's under house arrest for a crime she didn't commit."

The delivery boy cast her a wary look.

Scottie took the pizza box from him. "Don't listen to him. He's been locked up in his cage too long."

Will gave the delivery boy thirty dollars and told him to keep the change. "Geez, thanks," the boy said, backpedalling down the sidewalk. "Y'all have a nice night now."

Setting the pizza on the kitchen island, Scottie and Will dug in as though they hadn't seen food in days. Scottie peeled a piece of pepperoni off her slice and popped it in her mouth. "Okay, so let's hear it."

"Hear what?" he asked, stuffing half a slice of pizza in his mouth at once.

"Your reaction to the story I just told you. Just as you can read me, I can tell when something's on your mind."

"Let's forget about the Russian mob for a minute." He took a gulp of beer to wash down his pizza. "Aside from the fact that he lied to you, which we'll get back to in a minute, is this guy, Guy, a good guy?" He took another large bite of pizza. "Like who names their son Guy."

Scottie hesitated, nibbling at her pizza. "I thought so at first, but now I'm not so sure. I'm having a hard time being objective about him after he lied to me."

"See,"—he pointed his crust at her—"that's my issue with this whole thing. He didn't actually lie to you. He just withheld a vital piece of information about himself. And I gotta say, Scott, I probably would've done the same thing in his shoes. Hell, any man with an ounce of ambition would've done the same thing."

She let her slice of pizza drop to the plate. "So you're taking his side now?"

"Come on, Scottie. We're not in middle school anymore. I've never even met the guy, so of course I'm on your side. All I'm saying is that sometimes you set the bar too high for any human to live up to. Things are not always black and white. In this case, the way I see it, there's a lot of gray matter in the middle."

"What's that supposed to mean?"

"Most guys I know would've gone viral with those images

right away. But this guy didn't do that. He considered your feelings. Hell, he even went on this little adventure with you, to help you search for your mystery man."

"Only because his job depended on it. Don't get me wrong, Will. He wanted to identify this man as much as I did. Unfortunately, his reasons were entirely self-serving."

"Have you spoken to him since you left the beach?"

Scottie shook her head. "I blocked his number."

"That's real mature, sis." He gnawed on his pizza crust. "Maybe you shouldn't be so quick to judge. I haven't seen you looking all glowy in a long time. If ever." She rolled her eyes, and he added, "Seriously, you should see your face. You're shining like a million-watt lightbulb right now. I would hate for you to miss out on a chance for happiness over a simple misunderstanding."

26

AFTER SEVEN OR eight beers, Will declared himself too drunk to drive and stretched out on the sofa. "I hope you don't mind if I sleep here tonight."

"Why don't you get an Uber?" Scottie asked, more than a little tipsy herself.

"Because I have an early meeting in the morning and I need my car."

"Okay, then." She removed the afghan from the back of the sofa and spread it over him. "Thanks for the pep talk, Will." She tucked the blanket under his chin and kissed his forehead. "Sleep tight. And be careful not to let the Russian mobsters bite."

Scottie dragged her suitcase up the stairs and stopped outside nursery. The cleaning crew must have left the door open. She toured the room, smelling the baby powder on the changing table and giving the mobile of zoo animals on the crib a twirl. She brought the soft flannel blanket to her nose and sniffed the faint sweet odor of Mary that still clung to the fabric. She lay down on the daybed and curled up with the blanket. As soon as she returned from Rio, she would donate the baby furniture to Goodwill and paint her new office a dramatic color. Maybe eggplant. Or teal. On second thought, maybe a subtle gray like her rooms downstairs would provide the right atmosphere to calm her mind and allow her imagination to flow. She drifted off to sleep thinking of sleek Lucite desks and fluffy white shag carpet.

Scottie woke to the sound of the television in the family room below her, the smell of coffee wafting up the stairs. Footsteps pounded the hardwood floors and Will appeared in the doorway.

"We have a really big problem," he said.

"Let me guess." Scottie swung her legs over the side of the bed. "You have a hangover?"

"A hangover I can deal with." He crossed the room and pulled her to her feet. "You better see this for yourself."

He led her down the hall to her bedroom where he clicked on the television and tuned into CNN. The image of Mikhail Popkov kissing Catherine Caine filled the screen. The caption underneath read: *Senator Caine's Steamy Love Affair with Russian Mobster.* Will turned up the volume, and they listened to the morning show anchors rip the Democratic candidate to shreds.

Scottie went to the window, making sure the FBI agents were still stationed out front. The stakes in the dangerous game she was playing had just ratcheted up a hundred notches. And her life had become the biggest reward. Popkov would surely come after her now.

"I don't understand. Who would've leaked the images? No one had copies but me." The realization hit her like Barry Bonds striking a home run. "Rich! That asshole!" Scottie darted from the room and flew down the stairs to the kitchen. She found her iPad in her electronics bag and clicked on her messages. Sure enough, yesterday during their meeting, Rich had texted the images to a Washington number, presumably his own, right before he deleted them.

"Who is Rich?" Will asked, joining her in the kitchen.

"Guy's coworker and partner in crime." Scottie explained how Rich had commandeered her iPad during their meeting yesterday. "He acted like he was doing me a favor by making sure they were deleted from the hard drive, but what he was really doing was texting the files to himself."

"How can you be so sure Guy was involved in leaking them to the press? Maybe this Rich dude acted on his own."

"Please, Will, don't start defending Guy again. You don't even know him."

"No, you're right, I don't." Will cast a nervous glance at his watch. "Listen, I hate to leave you alone in the middle of this crisis, but I can't miss this meeting. The division heads from all the different branches are coming in to discuss policy change. I'll be back around noon, as soon as the meeting is over. If you need me, call the main number and tell the receptionist you have an emergency and to interrupt me."

"Don't worry about me," she said, showing him to the front door. "I have plenty to do to get ready for my trip tomorrow. Anyway, nothing's going to happen to me with the President's Men guarding me." She opened the door wide, revealing the nondescript sedan parked on the curb.

"But I—"

Scottie gave her brother a gentle shove out the door. "Go to your meeting, and stop worrying about me."

She bolted the door behind him and went to the kitchen for coffee. She found her cell phone vibrating its way across the island with text messages and notifications of breaking news from several major networks. She picked up the phone. As she was scrolling through the messages, the screen lit up with an incoming call from a private number. She answered, "Scottie Darden."

"Please hold for a call from Senator Caine," a female voice said in a clipped tone.

Catherine Caine came on the line ten seconds later. "I trust you've seen the morning news. I thought we agreed you wouldn't release the photographs."

"We did, and I didn't. Trust me, Senator Caine, I have just as much to lose as you do. I don't know who is responsible, but I assure you, it isn't me."

"If not you, then who?"

"The GOP gets my vote." Scottie explained her theory about Rich Cartwright. "I'm so sorry, Senator. I wish I'd never taken the photographs in the first place." Her voice shook with unshed tears.

"I do too, Scottie. But I learned a long time ago not to waste good energy worrying about things you can't change." An awkward moment of silence fell between them. "If everything I've heard about Popkov is true, and I have no reason to doubt the FBI, this new development places you in a dangerous position. Do you have protection?"

"Yes, ma'am. There are two FBI men stationed outside my house as we speak."

"Well," the senator sighed. "I guess all we can do now is damage control. I've got a call in to Roger Baird. I'll let you know when I hear back from him."

"Thank you, Senator," Scottie said, and hung up.

She poured cream and sugar in her coffee, and then dropped down on the nearest bar stool. She tried to tell herself it didn't matter, but herself wouldn't listen. She needed to know whether Guy was in on the decision to leak the images. She unblocked his number from her phone. Several minutes later, a stream of messages appeared on her screen.

I don't know who did this, Scottie, but it wasn't me. Please believe me.

She texted back: *Rich did this. He texted the digital files to himself from my iPad during our meeting with the senator yesterday. I have the proof.*

A minute passed before he responded: *Thank God you unblocked me. I've been crazy with worry. I don't know what to say about Rich. I'm gonna drive down there so we can talk in person.*

Scottie: *Don't bother. The FBI won't let you in.*

Guy: *Please give me a chance.*

She went back into her phone settings and once again blocked his number. No matter what he said, she would never believe he had nothing to do with leaking the images.

Her phone rang again—Senator Caine calling back. "I've spoken with Baird, and we've agreed on a plan of action. I don't have time to explain right now, but in about an hour Baird and I will lay out our plan in a press conference, which will be broadcast on all the major networks. Popkov has no chance of getting away this time."

*

At noon, with her husband by her side, Catherine Caine held a press conference denying all accusations of an extramarital affair. She explained the situation as diplomatically as possible— that an overeager reporter had photographed a private meeting with a potential donor, a man Caine had never met but who promised a sizable contribution to her campaign. The senator turned the podium over to Agent Roger Baird who appealed to viewers to help the FBI locate this dangerous man. He outlined the charges Popkov faced and offered a substantial reward to anyone who could provide information leading to his arrest. Neither the senator nor the FBI agent mentioned her name, but by the time the news conference concluded, Scottie had been identified by social media as the overzealous paparazzo.

*

The FBI's sketch artist, Helen Joyner, arrived a few minutes past two. She was pretty and young, about Scottie's age, and very talented with a graphite stick. She declined Scottie's offer of iced tea and they got right to work.

As they settled in at the dining room table, Scottie said, "If you don't mind me saying so, using a pencil and paper to create the sketch seems archaic considering our modern technology."

Helen smiled. "Many police agencies use computer software programs designed specifically for this use. But the FBI believes the pencil and paper method produces more accurate results." She lined up several graphite sticks on the table alongside her sketch pad. "Now, tell me what you remember."

Scottie sat back in her chair. "His size is the characteristic that sticks out the most in my mind. He's huge, easily six and a half feet, if not taller, with massive hands. He could've choked the life out of the vice grip he held me in if he'd wanted to. I never really saw his face. He was behind me most of the time."

"Tell me any and every thing you remember about his face, no matter how big or small the detail," Helen said. "I need something to work with."

Closing her eyes, Scottie tried to summon an image. "His hair was pulled back in a ponytail, and he had a full beard on his long face."

"What color was his hair?"

"Dark, almost black, like his eyes," Scottie said.

"What shape was his nose?" Helen asked.

Scottie was unable to stop herself from smiling. "I'm not

sure what his nose looked like before, but after I broke it the other night, I imagine it is crooked now."

They went back and forth for more than an hour as Helen sketched out a reasonable likeness to the beast on her pad.

"I'm sorry for your ordeal, Scottie," Helen said on her way out. "I'll scan this composite into our system and see what matches we come up with. I'll be in touch."

*

Will stopped by with a bag of groceries around five o'clock, but much to Scottie's dismay, he'd made last-minute dinner plans with his out-of-town executives to continue their discussion on policy changes. Her bodyguards, the FBI agents stationed on the curb, checked in periodically, prior to and after every shift change. She was eating a salad for dinner when Kennedy and Nixon knocked on her door. They assured her there'd been no signs of Popkov and that arrangements had been made for her transfer to the airport the following afternoon. The President's Men checked on her again during their changing of guard at eleven, and Scottie went to bed right afterward with thoughts of the summer games occupying her mind.

At some point during the night, long after the bars had closed and the busy streets in the Fan had quieted down, two men broke into her house. She'd never seen one of them, but she recognized the beast, his beady eyes like black marbles leering at her from their purple sockets, the result of a broken nose. She was powerless to fight against their size and strength. They gagged her mouth, and duct-taped her ankles and wrists. The beast tossed her over his shoulders like a bag of horse feed and hauled her down the stairs and out the back of the house to a small moving truck parked in the alley. "You're gonna pay, bitch, for breaking my nose." He flung her onto the metal floor of the cargo compartment, and tugged a cloth bag over her head.

Scottie screamed into the darkness, but her cries were muffled by the gag. The night was quiet. Something was missing. What had happened to the Yorkie Terrors next door?

27

SCOTTIE HEARD THE truck door slam followed by retreating footsteps, the sound of one of them running away. The engine started and the truck began to slowly move, bouncing over the bumps and potholes in the alley. As soon as he hit the pavement of the adjacent street, the driver accelerated like an ambulance operator rushing his dying patient to the nearest hospital.

With her hands and feet bound, Scottie had no way to protect herself on the reckless ride. Every time the driver made a sharp turn, she was tossed across the hard metal floor to the opposite side of the truck. As they sped through Richmond, presumably on their way out of town, she rolled around like a steel ball bouncing off the walls of a pinball machine. Once the erratic driving leveled off, she realized they were probably on the interstate, headed someplace far from home. She listened intently for sounds from the passenger cab, hoping for a clue as to where he was taking her, but she heard nothing, not even the music from the radio.

She found a comfortable position, curled up on her side. As the reality of her destiny sank in, Scottie cried a river of tears, but her sobs could not escape the duct tape covering her mouth and the cloth bag over her head. She'd been kidnapped by one of the most dangerous men in the world. Best case scenario—he'd torture her, then chop her up into pieces and feed her to the sharks. Worst case scenario—he'd sell her to a wealthy foreigner who would turn her into a junkie and use her body to perform unimaginable acts. Either way, Popkov would make certain she died a painful death.

The drone of the truck's tires on the pavement eventually lulled her to sleep. She dozed off and on for what seemed like hours, until the driver slammed on the brakes and sent her crashing to the front of the cargo hold. Next came a long period of weaving and swerving, and by the time the truck finally slowed to a stop, every bone felt bruised and every muscle in her body ached.

Scottie heard the driver's door slam, then a screen door bang shut somewhere off in the distance. Sometime later—she didn't know whether it was minutes or hours—the sound of a car pulling up beside the truck invaded the silence. The engine died and the car door closed. The cargo door rolled open and a pair of strong hands grasped her by the arms and hauled her across the floor.

"I warned you what would happen if you released the photos." Popkov yanked the bag off her head. Licking his lips, his eyes traveled her body as he took in her pajamas—the shorty bottoms and see-through tank top. "We can finally finish what we started in North Carolina, except that now I won't give you the choice of whether or not to sleep with me."

"Mmmm." She tried to talk, but the tape prevented her lips from moving.

"Let's take this off,"—Popkov ripped the duct tape from her lips, peeling the skin off with it—"so we can see what you have to say for yourself."

Licking her lips, she screamed, "I said, I'm not the one who released the photos, you bastard!"

Popkov clamped his hand over her mouth. "Shh! You'll wake the neighbors." He laughed a menacing sound that made her blood run cold. "Oh, that's right. How could I forget? We don't have any neighbors way out here in the middle of nowhere."

The beast appeared at Popkov's side. "Sorry, boss. I didn't hear you drive up."

"That's all right, Felix. I was just welcoming our guest."

Felix grabbed Scottie and dragged her down from the cargo hold. He wrapped his powerful arms around her from behind, holding her tight, his hot breath on her neck.

Popkov tilted Scottie's chin. "Tell me, little one. Who leaked the photos if it wasn't you? Did your boyfriend have something to do with it?"

As mad as she was at Guy, Scottie shivered at the idea of these evil men hunting him down. "Leave him alone. This is between you and me."

"Calm down, little one. I have no intention of hurting your lover boy. He'll suffer enough pain when he realizes you won't be coming back."

"You won't get away with kidnapping me. The FBI is hot on your trail."

"Oh, sweetheart, I plan to get away with a whole lot more than kidnapping." He ran his finger down her cheek. "I haven't decided what to do with you. Whether to sell you or keep you for myself, although your mouth might get tiresome after a while."

Jutting her chin out, Scottie said, "You don't scare me."

Popkov slapped her hard across the cheek. "You'll be plenty scared of me when I finish with you. Felix, show our guest what sort of games we like to play."

With one arm holding her still, Felix produced a syringe with his opposite hand and jabbed a needle in her thigh. Within seconds, everything went black.

*

Scottie awakened sometime later, blinking her eyes into focus as she surveyed her new surroundings. A single lightbulb in the ceiling cast a dim glow over what appeared to be a basement room with cinder-block walls, a concrete floor, and no windows. A toilet stood in the corner of the room next to a single porcelain sink. Relieved to discover her wrists and ankles were no longer bound, she scrambled to her feet and scurried across the floor, anxious to relieve herself.

She wandered the perimeter of the basement, searching for a door or window, but the only way out appeared to be the iron staircase in the center of the room. She didn't need to climb the stairs to know the door at the top was locked. Her legs buckled and she dropped to the floor. Still groggy from the drugs, she curled into a ball and dozed off.

When she woke again, Popkov was standing over her, staring at her. She had no idea how long he'd been there.

"What did you inject me with?" Scottie asked.

"Nothing to worry about. Yet. That was just a harmless tranquilizer, but if you run your mouth or cause me any trouble, I will shoot you high with heroin and keep you there."

Scottie's skin crawled at the thought of poison pumping through her veins. She'd written a story about heroin addiction for the *Richmond Times Dispatch* a couple years back. During her research, she'd interviewed several recovering addicts. Prisoner or not, no way would she want to trade places with them, to fight that battle every day.

"I don't understand what you want with me," she said. "I'm

no longer a threat to you now that the photos have been released. Just let me go. I promise not to tell anyone."

"Ah… but you are the innocent one now, aren't you?" He lifted a lock of her hair to his nose and sniffed it. "It's all about revenge, my little friend."

Scottie flinched. "You'll never get away with it. Your face is plastered over every computer and television screen in the country. It's only a matter of time before the FBI finds you. You might as well book the next flight to Russia or wherever the hell it is you came from."

His lips curled into a smirk. "The FBI? What a joke. They've been chasing me for years. So far, they haven't come close to finding me."

28

THE FOLLOWING DAY, Guy met with some of his team members to discuss damage control. The fallout surrounding the leaked photographs of Caine and Popkov was presenting quite a challenge. Shortly before noon, he received a call from Roger Baird. "If you'll excuse me, I need to take this call," he said to those gathered around the table. He stepped out of the conference room. "Roger, can I call you back? I'm in an important meeting."

"I'm afraid this can't wait. Scottie's been kidnapped."

Fear crept up Guy's spine. "What? When?"

"Sometime during the night last night. She seemed fine when my men checked on her during their shift change at eleven."

"Are you telling me someone broke into Scottie's house and kidnapped her while your men were stationed out front?"

"That's exactly what I'm saying. To make matters worse, whoever kidnapped Scottie killed the two Yorkshire terriers that belong to the owner of the house next door."

"What the fuck, Baird? Were your men sleeping on the job?"

"Just calm down, Guy. I understand you're upset."

"You don't understand the half of it." He turned his back on the nearby campaign workers who had stopped what they were doing to listen to his conversation. "Where are you now?"

"A block away from your office building. On my way to Richmond. Want me to pick you up?"

"I'll meet you downstairs in five minutes." By the time Guy returned to the conference room for his things, then made the trip down ten flights in the slow elevator, Roger's black Yukon was parked illegally on the curb in front of his building.

"Start talking," Guy said as he slid into the passenger seat.

Roger turned on his blue lights and sped through the city center toward the expressway. "I'll be honest with you, Guy. Our men really screwed the pooch this time. Mistake number one, we had two rookie agents on surveillance detail. They reported nothing out of the ordinary during the night. When they rang Scottie's doorbell at seven this morning to notify her of a shift change, instead of following through when she didn't answer, they assumed she was sleeping and decided not to disturb her. One of them finally became suspicious around ten when the blinds remained closed in her bedroom. It appears as though the kidnappers parked in the alley behind Scottie's house and forced their way in through the French doors leading from her courtyard. Nothing appears to be missing. Her cell phone was still charging on the table next to her bed."

"What about her laptop and iPad?"

"All accounted for," Roger said. "As is her purse with her wallet and car keys inside."

Guy's stomach clenched and he felt like he might vomit. "Then she has no way of communicating with us."

"Affirmative."

"And these men killed the next-door neighbor's pets?" Guy asked.

"In cold blood. We figure there were two men. They would've had to kill both dogs at once to keep the other from barking."

"Have you contacted Scottie's family?"

"Her brother is on the scene in Richmond. Her parents, on the other hand, are celebrating their anniversary on an Alaskan cruise. They are somewhere between Anchorage and Sitka as we speak."

"Scottie speaks highly of her brother, Will. He should be of help."

Roger snorted. "From what I hear, Will is raising holy hell down there."

"And he has every right to be," Guy mumbled. "What's your plan of action?"

"We'll find out when we get there. If I have my way, we'll plaster this bastard's face on every news broadcast and across every social media site in the country."

Roger's cell phone rang and he answered it. For the rest of the drive to Richmond, Guy listened to the agent's one-sided phone conversations. Just as he'd start to ask a question, Baird's phone would ring again, interrupting him. Even so, Guy managed to piece together the important facts. None of the neighbors heard or saw any suspicious-looking persons or vehicles in the area during the time in question, not even the next-door neighbor whose terriers had been brutally murdered. No Jane Does had been admitted to any of the area hospitals. No ransom calls had come in as of yet, either at Scottie's home in Richmond or at her parents' farm out in the country. Scottie had disappeared without a trace.

Guy stared out the passenger window, his ears tuned in to Roger's conversations while his mind reflected on the last few days he'd spent with Scottie. He knew she was in danger, yet he let her go back to Richmond alone. Regardless of how mad she was at him, he should have followed her home and stayed by her side until the FBI had Popkov in custody. He understood the statistics. He knew the odds of finding a kidnapped victim decreased with each passing hour. With no eyewitnesses, the FBI had little to go on. Without the make and model of the vehicle the kidnappers were driving, the traffic and toll booth cameras were useless.

The reality that he loved Scottie, that he might have lost the woman who could make him happy, caused an agonizing pain in his heart.

He thought about the way she fingered the tendrils of curls along her hairline when she was deep in concentration, the way she smelled fresh like an early summer morning. He thought about her quick wit, and the way sparring with her made him feel alive.

When they arrived in Richmond, Roger drove past the street where she lived and turned into the alley that ran the length of her block behind her house. "I need to see this for myself." He maneuvered the potholes and came to a stop at the back of Scottie's house. They pushed open a tall wooden gate and entered her brick courtyard.

"That was too easy, Roger. You are going to have a lot of explaining to do."

"I'm aware." Roger straightened his shoulders and held his head high. "Here goes nothing," he said, and disappeared inside.

Guy chose to remain on the patio, letting Roger enter the lion's den alone. Guy's head was not on the chopping block. At least not this time.

He admired Scottie's charming courtyard. An iron table and four chairs were set up beside a grill on one side of the terrace while a teak bench sporting an arrangement of brightly colored pillows occupied the corner of the other. Planters in all shapes and sizes were scattered about with flowers spilling over the tops. Except that the flowers were looking kind of droopy, as though they hadn't been watered in a while.

Guy located a spigot on the side of the house and dragged the hose from planter to planter, giving each flower a healthy drink. He was coiling the hose back up when a man who could only be Scottie's brother, based on her description of him, came out onto the patio.

"Thanks for watering the flowers. It doesn't take long for them to wilt in this heat. I'm Scottie's brother, Will."

Guy accepted his outstretched hand. "Guy Jordan."

Will looked Guy over from head to toe the way most father's check out their daughter's dates. "So you're that guy."

Guy appeared surprised, even though he had no reason to be. He knew enough about Scottie's relationship with her brother to know they didn't keep many secrets from one another. "She told you about me, did she? Considering the situation, I don't imagine she had anything nice to say."

"It's what she didn't say that intrigues me," Will said.

Guy hung his head. "I didn't mean to hurt her."

Will leaned back against the house, crossing his arms. "Then why did you?"

"I made a bad decision for a good reason. I don't know how much she told you."

"Everything," Will said without hesitation.

"Okay, then. At least that makes it easy." Guy braced himself against the iron stair railing. "When Scottie came to me with the photographs, and I showed them to my coworkers, they were ready to release them on the spot. I talked them into giving me a few days. I felt it in everybody's best interest to identify the man in the photographs before we released them.

"*I* made the decision to go on the road trip with Scottie. No way was I going to let her go alone. The situation got more and more complicated as time went on. I eventually told Scottie that I worked for the Republican Party. I left out the part that I was one of the top organizers, because I didn't think it mattered. Of course she didn't believe me."

"She can be stubborn like that."

Guy gestured at the French doors, at the group of men gathered on the other side. "Are they making any progress in there?"

"Depends on how you define *progress*. They've decided to hold a press conference. The idea is to enlist the help of the American people in finding Scottie."

Guy shook his head in disappointment. "Because they have nothing else to go on."

"Exactly." Will opened the door and a wave of cold air rushed out. "You might as well come inside."

29

GUY WANDERED AROUND the downstairs rooms of Scottie's house, admiring her eclectic mixture of furnishings. The home reminded him of the person who resided within, her soft and loving side evident in the calm gray walls and carpet while her flair for the dramatic showed in the big punches of color from the art and fabrics.

He climbed the stairs to the second floor with apprehension. A part of him needed to see where Scottie last rested her head. Yet another part of him couldn't face the reality of what had happened to her in that room.

He never got beyond the nursery.

When Will found Guy thirty minutes later, he was still in the nursery in the rocking chair with a stuffed turtle clutched to his chest. "I thought you might want to know, the FBI will be starting the press conference in a few minutes."

"Great!" Guy tossed the stuffed turtle in the crib. "I can hardly wait to hear what those bumbling idiots have to say."

"They don't inspire much confidence, do they?" Will dropped down to the daybed next to Guy. "Scottie needs to clean out this room. Holding on to all this stuff isn't healthy."

"She told me about her miscarriages, and about Mary, but being in this room makes it all the more real."

"I'm surprised she told you about Mary," Will said. "She swore to keep that secret to her grave. She must really trust you."

"*Trusted*," Guy said. "As in past tense. She'll never forgive me for lying to her."

"Yes she will. Scottie never holds a grudge for long." Will got up and walked over to the crib, giving the mobile a hard push. "Scottie wants children more than anything. Who knows if she'll ever be able to have them?"

"She will. It's just not her time."

Will gave the mobile another solid punch, sending the zoo animals in one tangled mess to the mattress. "If Popkov has anything to do with it, she won't live to see another day."

Guy buried his face in his hands. "She's already been through so much. I should've protected her. I should've never let her out of my sight after we left the beach."

"I'm her brother. How do you think I feel?" Will rubbed his eyes with his balled fists. "I should've been here last night, and not at some business dinner."

Guy jumped to his feet. "I don't know about you, but I can't just sit around here waiting for the FBI to find her."

Will followed him out of the room. "I'm with you, man. Did you have anything specific in mind?"

"Not exactly," Guy said over his shoulder. "Why don't we start with the press conference and go from there?"

Guy and Will joined the crowd gathered in the front yard. The police had cordoned off the street, preventing cars from entering or leaving the block, and reporters had strategically placed microphones and cameras in front of Scottie's door waiting to capture Roger Baird's address to the nation.

Baird raised his hand to get the crowd's attention. "I'm going to make a brief statement, and then I'll take some questions." He paused for a moment while everyone quieted down. "The FBI owes photojournalist Scottie Darden a debt of gratitude for helping us crack the case in America's most wanted mystery man investigation. The photographs she shared with us led to the positive identification of a man we've been tracking for nearly a decade. His real name is Mikhail Popkov. He's a Russian immigrant who has been living in the United States illegally. He is wanted on charges of sex and drug trafficking, extortion, and murder. I'm sorry to report that Ms. Darden has now disappeared, believed to have been abducted during the night by Mikhail Popkov and his unknown accomplice or accomplices. Popkov should be considered armed and dangerous. We are asking the American people to help in the search for Scottie Darden. The FBI has provided photographs of Popkov and Darden to all major networks. These photographs are also available on the FBI website as well as a special website we've set up at bringscottiehome.com."

A flood of hands went up and Baird fielded several questions regarding Caine's association with Popkov. Finally, frustrated, he read from a notepad in his hand. "At a press conference yesterday, Senator Caine made a statement in which she denied having any sort of relationship with Popkov. According to the senator, one of her biggest supporters arranged the meeting with Popkov to discuss a potential donation to her campaign. She had no knowledge of his criminal activity at the time."

Guy's hand shot up, and Baird pointed at him. "Mr. Jordan."

"You mentioned that you've been searching for this armed and dangerous man for nearly a decade. Considering all the resources the FBI has, how is it that Popkov has eluded you for all these years?"

"That's a good question. Popkov has used a series of aliases and disguises over the years. His identity is multilayered. The photographs Ms. Darden shared with us were vital in helping us connect a few dots, if you will."

Guy raised his hand again. "What's to prevent him from using one of his aliases to try and escape the country?"

"Nothing. In fact, we fully expect Popkov to go underground. That's why the sooner we can bring him in the better. As I mentioned earlier, all known aliases and photographs are available on the special website we've dedicated to bringing Scottie home. Newsrooms, please provide that web address on the bottom of our viewers' screens."

Guy's hand went up yet again. "Do you have any information regarding the escape vehicle?"

Baird's jaw tightened. "No, another good question, Guy," he said, his voice tinged with irritation. "We are going door to door in the neighborhood in search of anyone who might have seen a strange vehicle in the area last night between the hours of eleven and three a.m."

Guy was on the cusp of asking another question, one about the murdered pets next door, when Will leaned in and said, "Don't make him mad. We need him on our side."

Baird wrapped up the press conference, and Guy followed him back inside. He needed answers and he intended to get them. It wasn't until he had cornered Baird in the dining room that he realized Will was no longer behind him.

"Every second counts here, Baird," Guy said, getting so close to the agent's face he could smell the onions he'd eaten for lunch. "I'm sure I don't need to tell you that. But I need *you* to tell *me* what you're doing to find her."

"Everything within our power, Guy." Placing his hands on Guy's shoulders, Baird gently backed him up three steps. "We've tapped the phone lines here, and at Scottie's parents' farm. The traffic cameras are useless without some clue about the vehicle they are driving. I promise you, we'll follow up on every lead that comes in. It'll take an army of agents to investigate the case, but I'm confident something will turn up."

"Where are you planning to monitor these calls?" Guy asked.

"We'll keep a small team here, at Scottie's house. The rest of the calls will be directed to a call center we're setting up at headquarters in DC."

Guy's shoulders slumped. "What can I do to help?"

Baird thought about it for a minute. "Are you headed back to DC?"

"Probably." Guy hadn't thought ahead to the next step. "I want to be close to the call center."

"Can I schedule some time for you to work with our sketch artist on a composite of Popkov's assistant?" Baird asked.

Guy narrowed his eyes. "I thought Scottie already did that?"

"Scottie's composite led us to a dead end, unfortunately. We're hoping you can remember something she may have left out, a distinguishing mark like a scar or a tattoo."

"I'm not sure I have anything to add, but I'm certainly willing to try."

Will entered the room, slightly out of breath. "We have a lead." He waved a piece of paper in the air. "A friend of mine, an acquaintance really, approached me after the press conference. He saw a white cargo truck, like a small U-Haul moving truck without the logo, leaving the back alley around one o'clock last night."

Baird's eyes grew wide. "This might be the break we need. Bring him in here. We need to talk to him."

"You can't. He insists on remaining anonymous. He was visiting a friend last night when he spotted the truck. A friend his wife wouldn't necessarily approve of, if you know what I mean."

Will handed Baird the slip of paper. "This woman lives across from the entrance to the alley. My friend got a glimpse of the license plates—blue and gold, probably Pennsylvania tags, with the last four digits nine-eight-four-five."

Baird snatched the note from Will. "Good work." He slapped Will on the back. "We'll get on this right away."

When Baird darted out of the room, Guy turned to Will. "According to Baird, they are setting up the main call center in their headquarters in Washington. I'm heading back there now. Care to join me?"

30

G UY ADMIRED THE ease in which Will communicated with the staffers in the call center at FBI headquarters. These people were working hard to find his sister and he wanted to show his appreciation, to make their work easier. He joked with them in a way that lightened the mood without diminishing the seriousness of the situation. He remembered their names, inquired about their health, and commented on the family photos they had pinned to their cubicles. He brought up coffee and bagels from the kiosk in the lobby, ordered in pizza for lunch, and for a sugar boost mid-afternoon, he offered Krispy Kreme doughnuts and homemade cookies from the bakery down the street. His presence in Command Central was a constant reminder of their purpose. He showed them pictures of Scottie on his iPad, and told them stories of their life growing up on the farm.

The next big break in the case came on the afternoon of the second day. Guy instructed the sketch artist to make a few minor adjustments to Scottie's depiction of the beast—thickening the eyebrows, narrowing the jaw, and adding an angry-looking scar that crossed his forehead—which led to the positive identification of Popkov's thug. Born and raised in Beckley, West Virginia,

Felix Lightfoot never graduated from high school. His last known occupation was as a car mechanic in Texarkana, Arkansas. When the FBI issued an all points bulletin for Lightfoot and released the sketch to the national news networks, a new wave of calls flooded the call center.

The tips numbered in the thousands, and while the FBI took all of the calls seriously—aside from the ludicrous reports of alien invasions—they lacked the manpower to investigate each and every one.

Guy and Will put in eighteen-hour days, doing everything they could to help. They worked at night until eleven, and then grabbed a quick bite to eat and a beer on the way back to Guy's apartment. Guy never heard Will complain about the few hours of sleep he managed to clock on his sofa, but the exhaustion soon became evident in the dark circles under his eyes.

On their third night together, Will received a phone call from his parents and left the restaurant so he could talk in private. Guy watched him through the front window, pacing up and down the sidewalk, his shoulders hunched and his face pinched in concentration.

At the sight of his anguished face, Guy asked, "Is everything all right?" when Will returned.

"My parents finally managed to get off the cruise ship. They are in Seattle, boarding a plane for Washington as we speak." Will gulped down his beer. "You think I'm overprotective about Scottie. My dad is going to rattle more than one cage when he gets here."

*

Stuart and Barbara Westport arrived at Command Central mid-morning the following day, straight from the airport judging from their rumpled clothing. Guy could've picked Scottie's father out of a crowd, his resemblance to his daughter was so apparent in his sandy hair and blue eyes. Stuart wasted no time in dragging Roger Baird off to a nearby conference room, leaving Will to introduce his mother around to the staffers.

Barbara accepted Guy's outstretched hand with the same warm smile and brown eyes as Will's. "Guy Jordan is it? I believe I've heard a bit about you."

Guy's face beamed red. "Considering the situation, I don't imagine any of it was good."

"No one is casting any blame on you." Barbara's eyes glistened with unshed tears. "Don't get me wrong, I love my daughter dearly, and I'm terrified for her safety, but she would have gotten herself into this mess with or without your help."

"I'm concerned for her safety as well, Mrs. Westport. I haven't known Scottie long, but she means a great deal to me. She's an original."

"Thank heavens for small favors." Barbara tugged on her son's arm. "Don't you go getting yourself kidnapped. There's not enough mahogany hair color to cover my gray roots as it is."

Will wrapped his arms around his mother. "Don't worry, Mom. I'm perfectly fine sitting behind a desk all day managing other people's money."

He turned his mother loose, and before long she'd taken his place on the call center floor, asking questions and listening in on the calls.

Later on in the afternoon, Will pulled Guy aside. "Let's duck out of here for a while. I could really use a drink."

They snuck out of the office to an establishment across the street, a tavern with wood-paneled walls and red leather booths that had been around since the Kennedy era. They found empty seats at the bar and ordered Scotch on the rocks from the surly bartender.

"I can't do this anymore, dude," Will said. "Now that my father is here to herd the cattle, I'm cutting out."

Guy nearly choked on his drink.

"Easy there, man," Will said, smacking Guy on the back. "I mean that figuratively, you know? I hope you don't think I'm referring to the staffers as cattle."

"You don't say?" Guy wiped his mouth with his napkin. "I found it funny, because I used to be a cattle farmer. I grew up on a ranch in Wyoming."

"Well, I'll be damn," Will said, shaking his head in amazement. "My sister done found herself a cowboy." He leaned back in his seat and crossed his legs. He squinted his eyes as he studied Guy, as though seeing him in a whole new light. "I knew there was something different about you. You're not the run-of-the-mill, cut-from-pinstripe-cloth politician."

"Ha-ha." Guy drained the rest of his Scotch. "So now that you've had your laugh, big guy, where are you going?"

"To find my sister, because no one else seems to be capable of handling the job."

"How in the hell will you know where to look?"

Will removed a folded sheaf of papers from his back pocket and placed it on the bar in front of them. "I'm convinced they are hiding her somewhere in the Poconos." They studied the traffic-camera surveillance reports. "The cargo truck entered Pennsylvania, but there is no sign of it ever leaving. *And*,"—he flipped to a map he'd printed from the Internet—"there are two separate sightings, both from convenience store clerks, of a man matching Lightfoot's description, only five miles from one another. Here and here." He jabbed his finger at the two red Xs he'd marked on the map.

"When do we leave?" Guy asked.

Will looked up from the map, surprised. "Don't you have a

campaign to manage or something? I'm pretty sure you're going to get fired soon if you don't go back to work."

"I don't care if they do fire me. Nothing else matters to me right now, except finding Scottie."

Will signaled the bartender for another round. "Then grab your pistol and saddle up your horse, partner. We've got ourselves a manhunt."

31

TIME STRETCHED AHEAD of Scottie like the Sahara Desert, long and bleak and desolate. Without windows to offer sunlight and darkness, with only the dim glow from the ceiling bulb to cast shadows over her concrete prison, Scottie had no way of differentiating between daytime and night. Even though the meals Popkov brought her were all the same—sandwiches made from processed cheese on stale bread—the timing of the delivery offered the only structure to her existence. The shortest period in between sandwiches was from breakfast to lunch, followed by a slightly longer stretch before dinner. Nighttime was the hardest. The hunger pangs she experienced between dinner and breakfast kept her tossing and turning throughout the night.

Loneliness played tricks on her mind. She heard voices—her parents' and Will's and Brad's—taunting her, reminding her of all the bad decisions she'd made. She vacillated between clawing at the walls in rage and sobbing for long hours in self-pity. She was supposed to be at the Olympics in Rio de Janeiro. Instead, she was being held hostage by a lunatic who planned to torture her to death. Hadn't she suffered enough during the past two years with three miscarriages and a failed marriage?

Popkov appeared alone when he brought her meals, but she sensed Felix lurking in the shadows at the top of the stairs. The Russian mobster didn't care to get his manicured hands dirty. He left the stabbing and shooting and bone breaking to his thug.

She asked for things—a blanket, a toothbrush, something to tie her hair back with—but Popkov refused her requests. It creeped her out the way his eyes roamed her body, the way he brushed her hair off her face and ran his finger down her cheek. She didn't dare think about what he had in store for her.

On her second day in the basement, during one of her many searches for an escape route, she discovered a trapdoor in the concrete, painted the same drab gray as the floor and walls. Beneath the hatch, she found human bone—skulls and femurs and humeri.

Scottie gasped. *I sure as shit do not want to end up like these poor women, forgotten forever, my bones buried in some dank basement. I need a plan and fast. If I don't fight my way free, these maniacs will make sure I suffer.*

When Popkov delivered her sandwich that night, she begged him once again to set her free. "Just let me go. I'll never say a word to the authorities. I promise."

He tucked a finger under her chin and lifted her face to his. "Stop torturing yourself, my little one. The sooner you accept your fate, the better off you'll be. You belong to me now. A lot depends on your behavior, of course. But the choice is mine whether you live or die."

Scottie took a step back from him. "You might as well kill me now and get it over with, because I have no intention of making nice to a loser like you."

His jaw tightened. "You need to learn to control that fiery temper of yours. If you don't obey, I'll be forced to make your loved ones pay." He held his cell phone up for Scottie to see the photograph of her brother and Guy standing together in what appeared to be her front yard. When she grabbed at the phone, Popkov jerked it away from her.

"Leave them alone, you bastard. They have nothing to do with any of this." Scottie sank to the floor. She was no match for this lunatic. If she didn't obey, Popkov would kill Guy and Will, all because of her.

She couldn't let that happen.

To keep up her strength, Scottie ate every crumb of the stale cheese sandwiches he brought her. She did jumping jacks and push-ups and planks—hardcore workouts she'd learned in her exercise class at home. She contemplated the crippling blows she'd learned in her self-defense class and practiced the few karate moves she remembered from the lessons she and Will took when they were young. She worked up a sweat, and with no clothes to change into or soap to wash her body, she could barely tolerate living in her own skin. But that only made her work harder.

She took to spending long hours sitting at the top of the stairs eavesdropping on her captors on the other side of the door. Over time, she learned their habits. The house was mostly quiet aside from the constant drone of sports anchors commentating on one baseball game after another. She suspected Popkov lived somewhere else, somewhere close by, and she began to anticipate his visits by the sound of his car in the driveway, followed by the opening and closing of the front door. After his arrival, a hushed exchange took place between the two men for several minutes before Popkov's visit to the basement. On most mornings after breakfast, she heard the sound of a louder engine in the drive-way—the sound of Felix leaving in the truck—and the reporting on the television switched from sports to news. With her ear pressed to the door, Scottie listened intently for any information regarding her disappearance. But she heard nothing. As far as she could tell, no one even knew she was missing.

At night, as soon as Popkov left after the evening sandwich delivery, Felix made frequent runs to the back of the house, to the room beside the basement staircase—a kitchen judging by the sound of the refrigerator door opening and beer tops popping. After ten or twelve of these trips, the stairs above her groaned under the pressure of Felix's enormous body as he lumbered up to bed. How easy it would've been for her to slip out at night while Felix was asleep. She tried everything, prying the hinges and picking at the lock and throwing her weight against it, but the door wouldn't budge.

She was desperate for an escape plan, but with only her bare hands as a weapon, all her ideas seemed futile. Then, during one of Popkov's sandwich deliveries, when he knelt down beside her to caress her arm, she caught a glimpse of a revolver strapped to his ankle. She knew how to handle guns. She'd learned to fire a pistol when she was a little girl. She'd blown countless Coke cans off tree stumps, and visited the local firing range many times. She'd been on bird hunting trips with her father—shooting doves, ducks, and geese. Hell, she'd even killed an eight-point buck with her bow and arrow. But whether she could take another human's life—even if it meant saving her own—remained to be seen.

She only hoped she wouldn't have to find out.

32

"IS YOUR DAD pissed at you for leaving Washington?" Guy asked when he and Will were headed up Interstate 95 in Will's pickup truck.

"Hell no. Not my dad." Will aimed his thumb at his chest. "My dad shoved a wad of twenty-dollar bills at me, gave me a big hug, and told me to kill the bastards if I got the chance."

Guy snickered. "Sounds like my kind of man. What about your mom? What did she say?"

"She told me to bring Scottie home as soon as I could so she could turn her over her knee." They both laughed, then Will's face turned somber. "I've only seen my mom cry a handful of times in my life, but she hasn't stopped crying since she got off the plane yesterday morning."

"I didn't see Baird before we left the office, did you?" Guy asked.

"No, and I wasn't looking for him either. I honestly doubt he would be in support of our vigilante manhunt."

When Will opened his center console for his sunglasses, Guy caught a glimpse of a pistol. "Dude, seriously? I can't believe you are packing heat."

"Damn right. I'm prepared for when we come face to face with Popkov," Will said, his voice full of hatred.

Guy lifted the holster out of the console. "This is a sweet piece," he said, admiring the stainless steel Ruger. "How long have you had it?"

"I bought it last year, when it first came on the market. It's lightweight and easy to fire."

Releasing the magazine, Guy noted that the pistol was fully loaded. "How many rounds does it hold?"

"Fifteen per magazine." Will felt around inside the console. "There's another magazine in here somewhere." He found the cartridge chamber and handed it to Guy.

"You're not messing around now, are you?"

"Damn straight. I won't think twice about putting a bullet between Popkov's eyes, if it means saving my sister's life."

Will and Guy rode for most of the four-hour trip in silence, each lost in thoughts of what-ifs and what-if-nots. When they arrived in the Poconos close to midnight, they checked in at the two convenience stores—the Minute Market and the Country Store—where Felix Lightfoot had been spotted. The night clerks at both establishments instructed them to return at seven to speak to the morning attendants. Too tired to keep their eyes open, they checked into a nearby roadside motel where they grabbed a few hours sleep—fully clothed on top of the tattered bedspreads. When Guy's alarm sounded just before six, they brushed their teeth, pulled baseball caps down low over their uncombed hair, and returned to the trail.

The morning clerk, a fleshy woman in desperate need of dental work, was already behind the counter when they arrived at the Minute Market. Her name tag, Bobby Sue, confirmed that she was the employee they needed to speak with.

"Good morning, ma'am," Guy said. "If you don't mind, we'd

like to have a word with you about this man." He produced a copy of the character sketch of Felix Lightfoot.

She raised a penciled-on eyebrow. "You with the FBI?"

"Not exactly, but we're helping the FBI with their investigation," Guy said, and Will added, "My sister is the missing journalist they've been talking about on the news."

She eyed Will up and down. "Ain't that a pity. Pretty thing, your sister. She should learn where not to point her camera."

Will's jaw tightened. "Fu—"

"What can you tell us about this man?" Guy waved the sketch in front of the woman's face before Will could finish.

"I ain't seen him today. He usually comes in around ten thirty or eleven."

Will's body tensed. "You mean he has come in more than once?"

"Yep. Nearly every other day for as long as I've worked here."

"So he lives in the area, as far as you know?" Guy asked.

She shrugged. "Only thing that makes any sense to me."

"Did you tell this to the FBI?" Will asked.

"Nah, they didn't ask."

When Will's face flushed with anger, Guy nudged him toward the back of the store. "Why don't you go find us some coffee? I like mine black." Guy leaned back against the counter and crossed his arms over his chest. He waited until Will was out of earshot before he said, "So... Bobby Sue... you said this Lightfoot character usually comes in around eleven?"

"Yep, that's right." She unwrapped a stick of chewing gum and crammed it in her mouth. "Ten thirty, eleven, sometime around then."

"Does he ever come in during the afternoon or at night?"

"I wouldn't know. My shift ends at three."

"Have you discussed him with your coworkers?"

"Nope, but you're welcome to come back at three and talk to Patsy. She manages the shift after me."

Guy wondered how much managing a one-person shift entailed. "You've been very helpful. If it's all right with you, we're gonna hang out for a while in our truck in the parking lot, to see if he shows up."

"Fine by me, as long as you don't go harassing my customers."

When Will approached the counter with two large coffees, Guy removed his wallet and handed her a ten-dollar bill. "Keep the change."

She smiled at Guy, revealing a gaping hole where her canine tooth once belonged.

"God damn it!" Will pounded the steering wheel when they got back in the truck. "I don't know who I'm more pissed off at, her or Baird."

Guy sipped his coffee. "You can't really blame her. She did her civic duty by reporting Lightfoot to the FBI. It's Baird's fault for not following up on the leads, especially since we have two convenience store clerks within five miles of one another reporting sightings of Lightfoot."

"You're right. I'm calling that bastard." Will keyed the number on his cell phone. "Agent Baird, this is Will Westport."

Will explained the situation to Baird, then held the phone away from his ear so Guy could hear Baird reprimanding them for taking matters into their own hands. Ending the call, Will slammed the phone down on the dashboard. "The bastard all but ordered us to come back to Washington. I'm sorry, man. But I can't do that. This is my sister we're talking about."

"You don't need to convince me, Will. I'm in this with you until the end."

Will's cell phone rang and he snatched it up off the

dashboard. He listened for a minute before he muttered his thanks and hung up. "They're sending a team to Pennsylvania, but they won't get here until tonight. In the meantime, Baird cautioned us to be careful, not to try to be heroes."

"Right. Like we're just gonna sit here and twiddle our thumbs while Popkov tortures Scottie right under our noses."

Will winced.

"Sorry, bro. That was in poor taste," Guy said.

Will hung his head. "You were merely stating the truth. It makes me crazy with rage to think about the bastard torturing my sister somewhere close by, and we can't get to her to help."

"Let's try to stay focused on the search."

"Fuck Baird. We're dealing with the local police from now on." When Will tipped his cup to his lips, coffee dribbled down his chin onto his shirt. "Damn it. Nothing is going my way today." He held the dripping cup away from him. "There should be a towel in the back somewhere. Can you hand it to me?"

Guy searched through the sports equipment on the floor in the back behind the driver's seat. Amongst the swim goggles, Frisbees, and balls for every kind of sport, he found a beach towel wrapped around two bottles of sunscreen. "Dude, what do you need all this stuff for?" He handed Will the towel.

Will mopped the coffee off his chin. "What can I say? I'm an active guy. I like to be prepared for wherever my day might take me."

Guy returned to the store for a bag of Sweet Sixteen Donuts and a stack of newspapers—*The Wall Street Journal*, *Washington Post*, and *USA Today*. Both men, each keeping an eye glued to the front door of the convenience store, spent the next several hours reading the papers and communicating with their respective offices via their cell phones.

Mainstream media was blaming the Republican Party for

Scottie's kidnapping, saying she would not have been placed in danger if certain members of Blackmore's staff hadn't irresponsibly leaked the photographs of Caine and Popkov with the sole intention of smearing the senator's reputation. Guy had not spoken to James or Rich since the story broke. They'd gone dark, refusing to return his calls and texts. He understood from his other coworkers that Blackmore was making heads roll, but so far, Guy had yet to hear from the GOP candidate. He wasn't sure whether that was a good or bad sign.

Finally, around noon, Will gave up. "Let's go down the road to the Country Store." He started the engine. "Maybe someone down there can shed some light on the situation."

The day clerk at the Country Store took one look at the sketch and said, "You just missed him. He was in here 'bout an hour ago."

"You're shitting me," Will said, unable to contain himself. "Are you sure it was him?"

"It was him alright," the clerk said. "I know this guy. He comes in here all the time. He's a real prick, if you know what I mean."

"How so?" Guy asked.

"He just ain't got no personality. He grunts if you try to talk to him. The other day he got all pissed off because we didn't have any fried chicken legs left, only thighs."

"Do you have any idea where Mr. Personality lives?" Guy asked.

The clerk shrugged. "Around here somewhere."

"I can't believe this shit." Will burst through the plate glass door and out into the parking lot. He paced around in circles in the empty space beside his truck. "I can't get over how ignorant these people are. What sane person allows a fugitive to live in his neighborhoods and shop in his stores? Mr. Personality, my ass. This man's a hardened criminal wanted for murder."

"Calm down, Will." Guy stepped in his path. "I know you're upset. None of this makes any sense to me either. But the last thing we need to do is call attention to ourselves. You never know who might be watching. Let's get back in the truck and call Baird. But you need to let me talk to him this time. You're too upset to be rational."

33

SCOTTIE SENSED HER time was running out. Popkov spoke to Felix in hushed tones for long periods of time during his visits. With her ear pressed to the door, she caught every third word of their conversations, enough to realize they were preparing to make a move. She wasn't sure whether they aimed to include her in the move or whether the move involved international travel. The FBI would never find her if her abductors somehow managed to smuggle her out of the country.

Her plan for escape was full of holes with no backup options if anything failed. She had no way of knowing if anyone was even searching for her, let alone close to finding her. No doubt the FBI would be on the manhunt for Popkov, and with any luck her sketch had enabled them to identify Felix as the beast. She knew she could count on her brother to move heaven and earth to try and find her. But Will was not a miracle worker. In this situation, she feared she had only herself to depend on for survival.

When she heard Popkov mention crossing the border, she knew she could no longer wait.

Scottie heard the click of the door unlocking at the top of the stairs. She rushed to the sink and began to splash water on her face. When she sensed Popkov's presence behind her, she turned to face him, lifting her shirttail up to wipe her face, exposing a significant portion of her breast in the process. His eyes filled with lust as he zeroed in on her chest. She raised her knee and delivered a swift kick to his solar plexus. His face filled with surprise and he staggered backward, falling to the ground and gasping for air. She removed his gun from his ankle holster and shoved it in the waistband of her pajamas. She crouched down behind the stairs and waited. As expected, at the sound of the commotion, Felix came barreling down the stairs. With both hands, she reached between the rungs, grabbed his right ankle, and tripped him, sending him crashing to the ground. While her captors writhed on the ground, Scottie trained her gun on them and backed up the stairs, closing and locking the dead bolt behind her.

She had given little consideration to what she would do or where she would go once she'd escaped from the basement. She'd thought about hiding out in the woods until nightfall or following the driveway to the nearest road and signaling oncoming cars for help. The sight of Popkov's Porsche parked in the driveway presented yet another alternative. A quick search of the room produced his sport coat, and in the pocket of that coat, she found the car keys. She bolted outside and started the engine. She threw the car in reverse and spun around so that she was headed in the opposite direction. As she shifted the car into forward, she heard two loud explosions in immediate succession. When she slammed her foot on the gas pedal, the car jolted forward on two flat rear tires.

In her rearview mirror, she saw her captors hurrying toward her. She hopped out of the car, and with a steady hand, aimed the pistol at them. They stopped in their tracks. When Felix raised his weapon, Popkov shouted, "No, Felix! Hold your fire!"

Scottie released the safety, took aim at Felix's chest, and pulled the trigger. The clicking sound of an empty chamber brought a smile to Popkov's face. "You overestimated me, little one. Why would I need a loaded weapon when I have Felix?"

Fear gripped her throat, making it difficult to breathe. She glanced around, taking in her surroundings—the lake so large she couldn't see the other side and the dense woods encompassing the Cape Cod dwelling she had narrowly escaped from. If she ran, Felix would most assuredly shoot her in the back. She thought about screaming, and then realized no one was likely to hear her. Either way she needed to do something. And she preferred dying a quick death over the agonizing torture she sensed Popkov had in mind for her.

Felix made the decision for her. In three giant steps, he closed the distance between them and engulfed her from behind in his giant, muscular arms.

Popkov stood in front of her. He pressed his mouth over hers and forced his hot tongue between her lips. When she gagged, he slapped her hard across the face. "You'll regret this, you stupid bitch. I'm going to shoot you so high with heroin, you'll never want to come down. You'll be spreading your legs for me in no time, begging me for a fix."

Felix tightened his arms around her. "Should I take her back inside, boss?"

"No, you idiot. Those shots you fired are still echoing across the water. It's only a matter of time before the police arrive. Throw her in the back of the truck. We'll have to find another hiding spot until we're ready to leave the country. Or perhaps we'll drown her in the Hudson River and be done with her."

Popkov released the latch and rolled open the back door of the cargo truck. Felix swooped Scottie up in his arms and tossed her in the back like a sack of flour. When she scurried to the edge, Felix forced the door down, missing her legs by an inch. Once again she found herself in pitch darkness, right back where she'd started from.

34

GUY ENDED THE call with Roger Baird and pocketed his phone. "He's sending an army of people. Problem is, it will take them a while to get here."

"I'll believe it when I see them with my own eyes," Will said. "And what are we supposed to do in the meantime?"

"Baird wants us to find somewhere safe and wait for them."

"Like that's gonna happen." Will started the engine and pulled out of the parking lot, heading south in the opposite direction they'd come from earlier.

They drove aimlessly for several miles. When they passed a For Sale sign at the end of a long driveway, Guy ordered Will to turn around and go back.

"What for?" Will asked.

"I'd like to get a view of the lake," Guy said. "Pretending to be interested in the house we just passed that's on the market will give us that opportunity."

Will pulled off the side of the road, waited for several oncoming cars to pass, and then turned around. They drove down a long gravel driveway until the trees gave way to a clearing. The house was a quaint cedar-shake cottage with dormer windows and a wide front porch overlooking the water. Will parked the car alongside the house and they got out.

"Nice spread," Guy said, looking around. "Wonder how much they want for this place?"

Will cut his eyes at Guy. "Since when are you in the market for a lake house?"

"I'm retiring from politics, or didn't I tell you? I'm thinking about moving to the country and writing my life story."

Will laughed. "That's gonna be an awfully short memoir. How old are you, thirty?"

Guy shrugged. "My adventures with Scottie will take up several chapters."

"Oh no you don't. *Adventures with Scottie* is my story. I have enough material for a three-episode series."

They walked to the water's edge, then down the long boardwalk to the end of the pier. The lake was at least a mile wide with a shoreline that meandered off in the distance. Motor boats pulling skiers raced about while small sailboats zigzagged back and forth across the water.

Will leaned back against a piling and massaged his temples. "I feel utterly helpless." He spread his arms wide. "There are miles and miles of shoreline on this lake. Popkov could be holding my sister in any of these houses."

"Baird is on the way, and he's bringing a large team with him. They will canvass the area, door to door. We're close to finding her, Will. I feel it."

"I'm glad you feel it, because all I feel is angry. At Popkov, obviously, but at the FBI as well. Hell, I'm even a little angry at Scottie for not being more careful. Why'd she have to pick such a dangerous career? She'd be safer as a police officer."

"I have to respectfully disagree with you, man. She's your sister, and you know her much better than I do, but I can't imagine a girl with as much spunk as Scottie sitting behind a desk crunching numbers all day. She does what she does for a living because it suits her personality. I've seen your sister in action. I saw her break Lightfoot's nose, for crying out loud. She can take care of herself."

"Oh really?" He cocked an eyebrow. "Then explain to me why she's in this situation."

"She's in this situation because my coworkers acted irresponsibly by posting those images online. And the result was just as Scottie had feared." Guy looked away from him. "I'm willing to admit she makes an impulsive decision every now and then. But the results of those decisions haven't always been bad, have they?"

Will thought about it for a minute. "Pretty much, yeah. Her choices almost always lead to trouble. The safest place for Scottie is in Richmond, taking pictures of babies and brides."

Guy sat down on the edge of the dock. Tugging off his running shoes, he let his feet dangle in the water. "I haven't known her for that long, but I can't imagine Scottie being content as a wedding photographer. She wants to see the world, live on the edge. After three miscarriages and seven years of being anchored to a deadbeat husband, she deserves that opportunity. She needs to get it out of her system."

"And where exactly do you fit in?"

Guy locked eyes with him. "Any place she'll let me."

"You say that now, bro. You haven't been on Scottie's Wild Ride of Adventure for that long. But once you've been rocking and rolling for awhile, you'll be begging to get off. I would never abandon my sister, don't get me wrong. I just want her someplace safe, where I can keep my eye on her without risking my life."

"All I'm saying is, she'll settle down in her own time," Guy said. "Who knows? She might be ready after this episode."

Will hung his head. "Let's just hope she survives this episode."

"Keep the faith, my friend. She's going to survive." Guy lay back on the dock, letting the sun warm his face. "The weather is so pleasant up here in the mountains. Warm with no humidity. I'm tempted to take my clothes off and jump in the water in my boxer shorts."

"Go for it, dude. I'll try not to laugh when a realtor drives up with a prospective buyer."

They sat in silence for a while. Guy was putting his shoes back on when two loud successive pops echoed across the water. "Did you hear that?" Guy asked.

Will walked to the edge of the dock. "I did, but I couldn't tell exactly what it was. I'd guess fireworks or gunshots."

"Sounded like gunshots to me." Guy held his hand over his eyes, shielding them from the sun as he looked out across the lake. "If I had to guess, I'd say they came from somewhere over there." He pointed to a wooded area around the bend from them.

"Let's go check it out." Will sprinted down the pier, and Guy took off after him with one shoe on and one shoe off.

Will started the engine and peeled out of the gravel driveway. He hit the road and headed north in the direction of the gunshots. Lifting the lid on the center console, he removed his pistol and checked that the magazine was full.

"Okay, now drive slow," Guy said. "I think the sounds came from property somewhere along in here."

Will slowed to twenty miles an hour. About a half mile up the road, a white cargo truck sped out of a driveway in front of them, nearly tipping over on its side as it made the sharp turn moving in the opposite direction from them.

Guy caught a glimpse of the license plate. "That's them! That's Popkov! Turn this bitch around."

Will whipped the truck around and took off after them. Guy punched 911 on his cell phone and reported the situation to the operator. He used calm, measured sentences, but the urgency in his tone was undeniable. "We are headed south on Highway 31. The suspects are driving a white nondescript cargo truck with Pennsylvania plates, XLM nine-eight-four-five. We are right on their tail in a dark-gray Silverado pickup truck. Hurry! It's a matter of life and death."

Guy ended the call and dropped the phone in the cup holder. "Let's pray they respond. And fast."

Will handed his pistol to Guy. "You better hold this."

"Do you want me to try and shoot out one of their tires? I'm not a bad shot, but I'm better with a lasso in these situations."

"No, just hold on to it. The last thing we want to do is make them wreck, not with my sister in the back." His hands gripped tighter on the steering wheel until his knuckles turned white. "At least I hope she's in the back."

"I hope she's alive," Guy mumbled.

They drove for miles and miles along the curvy mountain road. There were no side streets offering escape, and with Will's expert driving, Lightfoot was unable to shake them from his bumper. "There's an intersection coming up," Guy said, studying the map app on his phone. "Highway 58. If we're lucky, the state police will use the opportunity to head them off."

Two minutes later they passed through said intersection, but there were no police vehicles, state or otherwise, waiting for them. They drove on for another few minutes until they caught sight of what appeared to be a roadblock ahead of them in the distance.

Slamming on the brakes, the cargo truck skidded out of control in front of them and careened off the highway into a tree.

"Oh fuck!" Will jerked his steering wheel, bringing his truck to an abrupt halt on the side of the road. "I sure as hell hope my sister survived that."

"Doesn't look like the driver did," Guy said, pointing at the blood splattered all over the driver's side window.

Popkov climbed out of the passenger side of the truck, appearing dazed and unsteady despite his tight grip on his pistol.

"I'm gonna kill that fucker." Will snatched his gun from Guy and jumped out of the truck. Guy grabbed the baseball back from the backseat and followed Will.

"Where's my sister, you bastard?" Will demanded, marching toward Popkov, his gun aimed at his chest.

The police sirens grew louder as they headed their way.

"Don't kill him," Guy called to Will. "Wait for the police. We need to keep him alive in case Scottie isn't in the truck."

Popkov pointed his weapon at Will. "He's too much of a coward to kill me."

"Don't count on it, mother fucker." Will leveled the pistol, took aim at Popkov's right shoulder, and pulled the trigger.

Popkov somehow managed to fire a round before stumbling backward to the ground. The bullet grazed Will, ripping a quarter-inch gash in the skin on his right upper arm.

"Shit! That stings," Will cried, grabbing his arm with his left hand.

"Here, give me that." Guy took the gun from Will and aimed it at Popkov. "I'll keep an eye on this asshole while you go see about your sister."

Will raised the door on the cargo hold. "Oh, thank God, she's here." Guy saw the tension leave Will's body. "And she's alive."

35

GUY DID NOT have a chance to say goodbye to Scottie before she left Washington the following morning. After missing a week of work, he needed to get to campaign headquarters as soon as possible to repair the damage to his job.

As he rode the Metro to the Capitol South station, he thought about the brief conversation he'd had with Scottie after the doctors finished checking her out at MedStar Washington Hospital Center the night before. She'd apologized for jumping to conclusions and not giving him a chance to explain about his job and Rich's text, and she'd thanked him for helping rescue her. But she'd offered little hope for any sort of future between them.

One lone tear had run down her cheek. "You don't want to be with me, Guy. I ruin everything I touch."

He'd rubbed her back and tried to assure her that she was still traumatized from her ordeal.

"Funny how things work out sometimes," she said. "Now that I actually have a shot at my dream job, I'm not sure that's what I want after all. In fact, I may never pick up a camera again. Turns out I'm not cut out for violence. Wedding photography is more my speed. There's no danger associated with taking pictures of brides and grooms on the happiest day of their lives. My life is a mess right now, and I need some time to figure a few things out on my own. Alone."

He'd begged her not to shut him out. "Why don't I drive you home to Richmond? We don't have to talk. I'll sleep in the guest room, or on the sofa. I won't ask anything of you that you aren't willing to give."

"It's not just about me needing to recover from my ordeal, Guy. I need to learn how to stand on my own two feet, to be responsible for my own actions without constantly dragging everyone I care about into my problems."

Of course he'd understood that. How could he not after everything she'd been through? "Take all the time you need. I won't pressure you. Just promise me you'll give me a chance. We can be happy together, you and me."

She'd turned her head away from him then, unable to look him in the eyes when she broke his heart. "I don't think so. You and I are not right for one another. The sex was great, don't get me wrong, but you deserve someone better, someone without the baggage, someone who can give you the family you deserve." She'd traced his lips with her finger. "I'll never forget you, Guy Jordan. You made me feel special. You made me believe in myself. Because of you, I know I will find love again. One day. It just won't be now. And it won't be with you."

*

The receptionist greeted Guy with a thumbs-up for a job well done. "By the way, the boss wants to see you."

Guy went straight to Blackmore's office, and waited outside while his secretary cleared him to go in.

"Well, now. If it isn't the man of the hour." Blackmore looked up from the file he was reading. "Close the door and have a seat." He waited for Guy to get settled. "I'd like to hear your side of the story, to see how it compares with your coworkers'."

After he spilled out the Spark Notes version of the story, Guy said, "I'm not one to throw a friend under the bus, but in this particular case, Rich deserves it."

"I agree to a certain extent. What Rich did was wrong on many different levels. But, to his credit, he told me the truth about everything when he and I met two days ago. James, on the other hand, denied his involvement in the situation. I had to let them both go, for different reasons of course." Blackmore leaned forward in his chair and propped his elbows on his desk. "Tell me, how is Scottie? She's a tough young woman to survive such an ordeal."

"She's traumatized, as you can imagine, but she's lucky to have a supportive family to help her recover."

Blackmore's expression grew serious. "You know the media has been all over us, blaming us for leaking the photos and holding us responsible for Scottie's kidnapping. Fortunately, we are not the only ones suffering. The Caine campaign has taken a direct hit as well. Nothing makes me happier than to see my campaign rise in the polls. But smearing my opponent with negative publicity is not the way I prefer to do business. I fight fair, Guy. You should know that by now."

Guy rubbed his temples. "I understand, sir. I realize now, I should have come to you in the beginning for advice instead of trying to handle the situation on my own."

"Yes, you should have. But I applaud you for trying to do the right thing, nonetheless." Blackmore knitted his fingers together and twiddled his thumbs. "With the election in less than three months, we have a lot of work to do to repair the damage to my reputation. Starting with the debate on Monday. I'm going to need you to travel to Dallas with me."

"Me, sir?" Traveling with the candidate had always been Rich's job.

Blackmore smiled. "Yes, you. Now that Rich and James are gone, I'm promoting you to my number one man. Unless you'd rather I find someone else."

"Oh, no, sir." Guy sat up straighter in his chair. "I'm honored you would consider me for the job. I promise I won't let you down."

"I have faith in you, Guy."

Guy beamed. "Thank you, sir."

"You're welcome." Blackmore nodded his head at the door. "Now get out of here and get back to work."

*

Guy spent the rest of the morning responding to emails and getting caught up on campaign news. He was eating a hot dog in the park down the street when he received a call from Will.

"How's the arm, bro?" Guy asked, as he picked up the call.

"Dude, you should see it. The chicks are gonna dig this scar."

Guy chuckled. "I can always count on you to put a positive spin on the situation. Are you back in Richmond?"

"Yep. I deposited my parents and Scottie at their respective homes, and I'm on my way to my house now." Will sighed. "Listen, Guy, about Scottie. She's feeling overwhelmed, and her feelings for you are kind of freaking her out, but she'll come around eventually."

Guy's appetite vanished, and he tossed his half-eaten hot dog in a nearby trashcan. "So she told you she gave me the boot."

"She didn't have to tell me. It's written all over her face. She pushes people away when they get too close. That's how Scottie copes. She'll come running back once she realizes she can't live without you."

"Maybe. Maybe not. I don't think it's that simple, Will. This is about more than our relationship. Did Scottie tell you she's giving up her career as a photojournalist? She's planning to photograph weddings on a permanent basis."

"Woo-hoo," Will said, and Guy imagined him fist-pumping the air. "That's the most sane decision my sister has ever made."

"She won't be happy."

"But she'll be safe."

"Every investigation isn't a corkscrew rollercoaster," Guy said.

"True, but there are few rides on the merry-go-round when Scottie is involved." A few seconds of silence passed between them. "Don't worry, bro. Scottie just needs a little time to process her ordeal. She'll be back to herself in a few days, and raring to go for a ride on the Tilt-A-Whirl."

"I hope you're right, Will."

"I usually am where my sister is concerned. Whatever you do, don't give up on her. Scottie always thinks she knows what's best for everyone else, but rarely does she realize what's good for herself. The most important thing right now is for her to know she's not alone."

*

Although he found the office much quieter without Rich's unrealistic demands and James's loud mouth, Guy had a hard time concentrating when he returned to work from lunch. He couldn't stop thinking about Scottie. She had every right to feel down about her life, considering everything she'd been through. Not just the kidnapping, but all the tribulations she'd shared with him about her personal life. He knew she felt something for him—Scottie wasn't the kind of girl who could fake anything— but he also understood how those feelings might terrify her so soon after her marriage had ended. No wonder she was confused when you factored in the uncertainty about her career.

Guy pondered what Will had said on the phone about Scottie—about her having a hard time realizing what's good for her and needing to know she's not alone. And the words began to resonate. She needed Guy, even if she didn't know she needed him. And he wouldn't let her down. He'd never felt this way about a woman before. He believed in his heart they belonged together. She was his hope for a happy future, and he couldn't let his big chance slip away.

Around three o'clock, Guy left his desk and returned to Blackmore's office. This time his secretary wasn't standing guard. He knocked on the open door.

Blackmore's eyes traveled from his computer to Guy. "You again so soon?"

"Yes, sir. If I might have a quick word."

Blackmore glanced at his watch. "That's about all I have time for. I have a meeting in five minutes."

Guy approached Blackmore's desk when he entered the office, but he didn't sit down. "I know I've missed a lot of work this past week, and I promise to give you one hundred percent from here on out, but I have a personal matter I need to attend to this afternoon."

"Does it concern Scottie?"

"Yes, sir. We… well, we have some unfinished business."

"I'm a family man, Guy. Who am I to stand in the way of love?"

"Thank you, sir," Guy said, but he remained rooted to the spot in front of Blackmore's desk.

"Well, what are you waiting for? Get out of here. Take the rest of the day off. Tomorrow too, if you need it. But I need you back in the office by Thursday. We have a lot of work to do before Dallas."

"I promise I won't let you down, sir. You can count on me."

Guy slid his computer and several files into his leather shoulder briefcase and headed out of the office, stopping by the receptionist's desk to alert her of his plans. For a brief moment, he considered going straight to CarMax and purchasing a used car, but the impulse passed quickly, and he decided to move toward buying a car in a more sensible manner. He would need a car with all the road trips to Richmond he had in mind for his future.

36

AT HOME IN Richmond, against her family's pleas to stay, Scottie insisted they leave, but she missed them before Will's truck had pulled away from the curb. She wanted to be alone to sort through her emotions, but she dreaded the demons that awaited her inside.

Everything appeared neat and tidy on the surface, but the sight of water rings on the granite countertops and dishes returned to the wrong place in the cabinets provided tangible evidence that strangers had been in her house. A super-size box of Starbucks K-cups—a dark roast that she had tried before but found way too strong—stood beside the Keurig. On her patio the FBI men had even stubbed out their cigarettes in her planters—her flowers long since fried to a crisp under the brutal summer sun.

Scottie saw Brad in every room—sitting on the leather sofa in the den, frying bologna at the stove in the kitchen. She wasn't pining for her husband. She felt enormous relief that her turbulent marriage was over. But she needed time to mourn the loss of a relationship that had lasted for eight years, just as she mourned the three babies who had died in her wound.

Memories of Mary awaited her in the nursery upstairs, too

bittersweet for her to contemplate. She closed the door to the room, vowing for the thousandth time to clean out the baby things and turn the space into an office.

Flashbacks and sound bites from the night of her kidnapping greeted her in her bedroom down the hall. She stripped the bed of its sheets and kicked the balled-up linens down the stairs. She filled her tub with lavender-scented bath gel and water so hot she could barely stand it, then soaked until her fingers and toes shriveled up like prunes. Even naked and alone with the door locked, she couldn't escape the noises she thought she heard and the vision of Popkov's face, a mirage that materialized in the steam. The knowledge that Popkov and Lightfoot would spend the rest of their lives in prison offered little consolation.

She dressed in clean khaki shorts and a pink T-shirt, braided her damp hair, and dabbed on a little makeup, hoping that the improvement in her appearance would improve her mood as well.

She cleaned her house from top to bottom—vacuuming and wiping away all traces of the intruders. She was starving when she finished around three, but a quick inspection of her refrigerator revealed a brick of moldy cheese and half of a leftover hamburger in a Styrofoam container. She made a bowl of ramen noodles, took one bite, and pushed the bowl away.

Scottie had finally found the man of her dreams, but she loved him too much to drag him down with her. She was ruined goods. Divorced at thirty, three miscarriages with little chance of carrying a baby to term, career washed up before it ever got off the ground. She had nothing to offer a rising political star. Guy needed a perky socialite wife who would dedicate her life to furthering his career.

With tears streaming down her face, Scottie lay down on the couch and cried herself to sleep. She woke up four hours later.

She removed a Stella from the twelve-pack in the

refrigerator—leftovers from the FBI's stay in her home. She popped the cap and sat down in front of her computer. She navigated to the Chanello's website and ordered a large pizza with two different meats and three kinds of vegetables. Tempted by the 217 emails in her inbox, she clicked on her Gmail app and began sorting. After deleting all the junk mail, she started at the bottom and worked her way from oldest to newest, reading through the concerned notes from friends and requests for appearances on early-morning and late-night television talk shows. She had job offers from ten different news services, but the one that interested her the most had come in only two hours ago—an email from an executive at Reuters wanting to know if she would consider a position as international correspondent based out of their London office.

London? She pushed back from her desk and sipped her beer as she considered the idea. The thought of moving overseas excited her as much as it terrified her.

Her phone vibrated on the island with an incoming text from Will: *Can I come over after work?*

She texted back: *No!*

She saw that two voice messages had come in while she napped—one from each of her parents checking on her, begging her to come stay at the farm for a few days. Maybe moving to London was exactly what she needed to put some distance between herself and her family. She loved them dearly, too much to continue to drag them into her drama. She wanted Will to find a sweet girl, settle down, and give their parents the grandchildren they so desperately wanted. He couldn't very well do that with his sister attached to him like a noose around his neck. She'd already ruined their parents' anniversary cruise. They deserved to be carefree at this stage of their lives, not constantly bailing their daughter out of trouble.

She sent Will a second text, one that sounded a little less harsh: *I love you and I'm grateful to you for saving my life but you don't need to babysit me anymore. Go live your life. Be free, big birdie.*

Will: *I understand you need some space, but I'm your brother. You can't push me away like you pushed Guy away.*

She opened another beer and wandered around the downstairs, admiring the home she'd created. She wondered how one went about moving their belongings overseas.

An international correspondent. Her dream job come true. Nothing was stopping her now but her own fears.

Scottie jumped at the sound of the doorbell, spilling some of her beer on the hardwood floor. Case in point. How could she go into a war-torn country, with bombs going off all around her and bullets whizzing by her head, when the sound of the pizza man ringing her doorbell turned her into a shivering coward?

"What are you doing here?" she asked, stunned to see Guy standing on her front door stoop.

"We need to talk. Do you mind if I come in?"

"We said everything that needed to be said last night at the hospital," Scottie said, making no moves toward letting him in.

"No, Scottie. *You* said everything you wanted to say. *I,* on the other hand, still have a few things I need to get off my chest."

Scottie saw the Chanello's delivery car turning the corner and heading toward her house. "All right, fine. But first let me pay for my pizza." She brushed past Guy and went out to the street to meet the pizza man. She noticed an Enterprise rental car parked on the curb behind her Mini. What could be so important for Guy to rent a car and drive all the way to Richmond to see her? Hadn't she made it clear they didn't have a future together?

She gave the delivery man twenty dollars and told him to keep the change. Pizza in hand, she returned to the house. "You might as well come inside," she said to Guy as she passed by him on the sidewalk.

In the kitchen, she removed two Stellas from the refrigerator and handed him one. "Courtesy of the US Government."

He furrowed his brow in confusion.

"Never mind," she said. "Do you want to go out to the courtyard? It's less than a hundred degrees outside for the first time in months."

"I guess." He eyed the pizza box on the counter. "I don't want to interrupt your dinner or anything."

"It's a pizza. It'll keep," she said holding the door to the terrace open for him.

Scottie sat down in the middle of her wooden bench, leaving no room for Guy to join her on either side. He stopped to examine the dead flowers in her planters. "I watered them when I was here. But that was days ago. I guess no one else thought to take care of them."

"I'm pretty sure watering plants isn't in the job description of an FBI agent. Why are you here, Guy? I thought we settled everything last night."

He placed his beer on the brick steps and crouched down beside the bench. "I want to be a part of your life, Scottie. You were wrong last night when you said we don't belong together, because we do. I get you. And I think you get me too."

Scottie let out a deep breath she didn't know she'd been holding. "We talked about this in DC. You driving all the way down here to say it again doesn't change anything."

"You're not going to make this easy for me, are you?" He nudged her to move over, to make room on the bench for him. "What I didn't say last night is that I love you. In fact, I'm crazy head over heels in love with you. And I think you feel the same about me."

She looked away from him. "I won't deny that I have feelings for you. But those feelings are all jumbled up with my messed-up life. I am so exhausted from thinking about it all."

"And understandably so. Which is why I'm willing to wait as long as it takes for you to figure things out."

"That's the thing, though. I don't know if I'll ever figure things out, if my life will ever feel normal again. What if you wait two years, or however long it takes for me to get my head straight, and it turns out we're not right for one another after all?"

"That's a chance I'm willing to take." He set her beer on the ground, and took her hands in his. "There's no doubt in my mind that you're perfect for me. I've never felt about anyone the way I feel about you. I love your sexy body, your inquisitive mind, and your sarcastic sense of humor. I love the way you furrow your brow and scrunch up your nose when you're deep in thought. And I love lying in bed in the dark with you, sharing our secrets and our dreams. Don't get me wrong, I love doing other things in bed with you as well." He brought her hands to his lips and kissed her fingertips. "I respect your need for adventure, your need to travel the world. And I promise you I won't stand in your way. I won't cramp your style."

"What if I told you I've been offered a job with Reuters and they want me to move to London?" Scottie watched closely for his reaction. His face registered surprise at first, and then he broke into a genuine smile that made his eyes sparkle.

"That is so awesome," he said, offering her a high five. "Your dream job come true. You deserve it. You've worked hard."

"Problem is, I never imagined my dream job would take me to London. Reporting on a story in Europe is one thing. Moving there permanently is a whole other matter."

He was silent for a minute, deep in thought. "Maybe I'll move to London with you. That is, if you want me to of course.

Depending on how the election goes, I may not have a job come November anyway."

She stared at him dumbfounded. She never thought he'd consider moving across the ocean just to be near her. "How would you earn a living? I don't imagine there are too many job opportunities in Great Britain for an American politician."

"Maybe I'll write a book." He mimicked typing on a keyboard.

"You mean, like a novel?"

"Maybe. Or a nonfiction perspective on what's wrong with our political system and the country as a whole. The critics can only hurt me but so much if I'm all the way across the ocean. I could get a job bartending or waiting tables to pay the rent."

"No offense, Guy, but I've been there and done that." Scottie got to her feet and crossed the courtyard, kneeling down next to the flowerbed that bordered her brick terrace.

Guy came to stand beside her, watching her as she pulled weeds. "It's not fair for you to compare me to Brad. We are two entirely different people."

"Fair or not, the reality is, I don't know you well enough to know whether I can trust you. Whether I can count on you to keep the promises you make. So far you're one for one. You withheld certain information about your career from me, but then you went out on a limb to help my brother find me. I honestly don't know what to think about you."

"I guess that's a risk you'll have to take. Life does not come with guarantees."

"What happens if Blackmore wins the election and offers you a White House job? You can't turn that down," she said, yanking up a clump of weeds. "And I wouldn't want you to."

"Then we'll try the transatlantic commute. We can Skype every night. I've always wanted to have cyber sex."

"That sounds like a barrel of monkeys." She stood to face him. "What about children? You deserve to have a family."

"And we'll have one if that's what we decide we want. Based on what you've told me, getting pregnant isn't your problem. We can find a specialist who deals with high-risk pregnancies. If that doesn't work out, we can adopt or hire a surrogate. These are problems couples face together, Scottie. This is what life as a married couple is all about, charting out our course together." He tucked a strand of hair behind her ear. "What do you say, sweetheart? Will you travel with me on my journey?"

The tenderness in his eyes made Scottie weak in the knees. Was she crazy to jump into another relationship so soon after the breakup of her marriage? And what about her dream job? Could she really ask him to come with her all the way to London? As she stared up into his handsome face, she knew she couldn't let him go. A part of her, maybe a bigger part of her than she was willing to admit, had already fallen in love with him. She wanted him to wrap his protective arms around her and never let go.

"I'm willing to give it a try, Guy. But that's the only promise I can make right now. If things get too complicated, I may need to ask you to back off."

He wrapped his arms around her. "That's fine by me. Consider yourself in the driver's seat. We'll take it slow or fast. Along the straight and narrow path, or down the rocky road, whichever you choose."

She took his face in her hands and kissed him tenderly on the lips. "In that case, fasten your seatbelt, Guy Jordan. It's gonna be a wild ride."

The End

AUTHOR'S NOTE

If I had my life to do over, I might consider a career in photo-journalism, a profession that would combine my two favorite hobbies—writing and photography. How exciting would it be to travel the world, capturing snapshots of history in the making? Part of the fun of being a fiction writer is exploring fantasy worlds. Which is exactly what I've done through the eyes of my protagonist, Scottie Darden. I hope you have as much fun reading about her as I had creating her.

I am working diligently on the sequel to *Her Sister's Shoes*, which I plan to publish late this summer. The saga of the Sweeney sisters continues in my revisit to the fictional town of Prospect, in the Lowcountry of South Carolina. The three Sweeney sisters—Jackie, Sam, and Faith—take on new challenges including a young newcomer who rocks their world.

ACKNOWLEDGEMENTS

I'd like to express my gratitude to my wonderful street team for their continued support. To Mamie, for being such an avid reader and providing such valuable feed back. To Alison, for helping me stay connected to the world and for offering such great advice. To Cheryl, for being the best public relations person an author could ask for. To Ellen, for starting my day with your smiling face and positive attitude. To Jody, for buying more of my books than you can give away. To my mother, for being you. To Pat, my trusted editor, for accommodating my schedule and for keeping me honest. To Kim, for your amazing talents as virtual assistant. To my husband, Ted, for being my biggest fan. And to my readers, for making the hard work worthwhile.

I've dedicated *Breaking the Story* to my children, Cameron and Ned, whose close relationship was the inspiration for my story. Cherish every day with the ones you love.

If you enjoyed the book and have a moment to spare, please consider posting a short review on Amazon and Goodreads to share your thoughts with others...

Please visit my website for more information about my novels
www.ashleyfarley.net